In Memory Of

WILLIAM H. SAVEDGE JR.

THE HORSE CAMP

Lew Palmer, Reg Bentley and Tom Lee went down into the Arizona Strip to trap wild horses. They caught fifteen, but mysterious strangers freed them in the night—the mustangers went looking for the strangers. What they found was a band of renegades, a wagon loaded with gold, silver and jewelled articles, and some crates of guns. They also found trouble and nearly got killed. Even after they escaped, strangers caught them in the night, and this time made them lead the way back to the renegade camp . . . All in all, it was quite an educational experience for Lew, Reg and Tom. What they learnt was that mustanging could be hazardous to their health.

THE HORSE CAMP

Nevada Carter

A Lythway Book

CHIVERS PRESS
BATH

First published in Great Britain 1986
by
Robert Hale Limited
This Large Print edition published by
Chivers Press
by arrangement with
Robert Hale Limited
1987

ISBN 0 7451 0565 3

British Library Cataloguing in Publication Data

Carter, Nevada
   The horse camp.—(A Lythway book)
   Rn: Lauran Paine I. Title
   813'.54[F]   PS3566.A34

   ISBN 0–7451–0565–3

Photoset, printed and bound in Great Britain by
REDWOOD BURN LIMITED, Trowbridge, Wiltshire

THE HORSE CAMP

CHAPTER ONE

TRAPPED

They had explored the territory in all directions for about thirty miles, but Tom Lee knew it best because he had grown up not very far from where they had decided to make camp. In fact it had been Tom's idea to establish the camp above the cul-de-sac canyon even though that meant they had to go almost two miles to water the horses, and bring back their own drinking water by the canteenful.

The lean, tanned blond rider with the slightly hawkish features named Lew Palmer did not like the idea of hauling water, but he did like being high enough so that they could keep watch over the endlessly broken, boulder-strewn, raw and uninhabited countryside where they had encountered abundant sign of wild horses.

The third man was a Canadian. How he happened to be in the Arizona Strip was an involved tale which he rarely referred to. Like Palmer, he was a sinewy, blue-eyed, hard-bitten individual, not particularly unusual in appearance except perhaps for a square jaw and an uncompromising general look. His name was Reg Bentley.

1

Tom Lee was a large man in his late twenties, with a fair complexion which burned and peeled on the desert, pale blue eyes, and a slightly clubbed left foot. The deformity was not noticeable unless he trotted or ran, things which he rarely had to do; no rangeman hastened on foot unless he could not find a horse to do the hurrying for him, and Tom Lee had always had horses close by.

He was a product of Utah; rugged, big-boned and well-muscled. He smiled a lot, was accustomed to being teased, and was normally easy-going and good-natured. Like his companions, Tom had never known luxury, and had only rarely known comfort or conveniences.

He stood in the shade of a stunted juniper where the drying desert breeze blew past but where he was somewhat protected from direct sunlight, and squinted at the desolate high desert on all sides. They were ninety miles from the nearest town—which was up in Utah. In the opposite direction they were at least four times that far from an Arizona town. In fact the only way to reach their camp in the Strip, was up into Utah, then southward back down into Arizona. It could not be reached from Arizona without considerable, and prolonged, hardship. For one thing there were no roads through the area, except the one which skirted the wild-horse country and entered Utah near Zion National Park, and where that skirted around above the high desert camp, was ninety miles northward.

Tom Lee, who did not smoke, watched Lew and Reg roll and light cigarettes at the nearby camp, and raised a big arm to gesture with as he said, 'It's no different from when In'ians owned it.'

Neither Lew nor Reg commented, although they glanced around where Tom was gesturing.

He dropped his arm and left the juniper shade to hunker down at the camp and pick up a canteen. Later, wiping his chin he said, 'They'll come and we'll catch 'em.'

Reg eyed the big Mormon. 'It'll take a while for them to smell the block salt.'

Tom was one of those people who had known so few real joys in life that when he imagined one, he would not relinquish the idea of it. 'We're not goin' anywhere,' he told Reg Bentley. 'We got the grub, the waterhole's not too far off . . . You own a watch, Reg?'

'No.'

'You own one, Lew?'

'No. What of it?'

'That's it, y'see. Time don't have to mean anythin' to us, does it? We just set up here and keep watch until the horses go into that blind canyon after the salt.' Tom's pinkish face creased into a broad smile. He looked from one of his companions to the other one as though expecting to be commended for his prescience. Instead, they sat like buck Indians smoking and

3

saying nothing.

There were a few fat clouds drifting from west to east, otherwise they were in a land without sound or movement. A man could have stood upon their barranca and yelled himself hoarse and except for a few lizards, some rattlers, maybe an occasional little desert fox or a mangy coyote, there would be no listeners. It was indeed as Tom Lee had said, no different than when the Indians passed through, or made camps near water now and then. But the Indians had not remained. It was too poor a country even for them.

It had a redeeming factor: wild horses. But even they would arouse little cupidity. For one thing, with wild horses, there are only two kinds, studs and mares. For another thing, since the Spaniards had brought horses to the New World, and some had got free to roam wild in the Southwest, they had been inbreeding. After several hundred years whatever quality the Spanish horses may once have possessed, they had lost generations ago. Mustangers had a saying about the animals they tried to catch which summed it up adequately. Wild horses were too small for men and too mean for kids.

Now and then a rare showing of quality appeared, but horse-catchers might sift through two or three hundred head of the treacherous little mangy bastards before seeing it, and generally, tough though the animals were, if

4

they exceeded eight hundred pounds or maybe twelve or thirteen hands in height, it was a miracle. A man who might weigh a hundred and sixty pounds riding a saddle which weighed somewhere between thirty and fifty pounds, required an animal under him whose hind feet didn't scuff sand and pebbles inside his boots, because it was too close to the ground and too light to pack him properly.

But, and this was the crux of the mustanging business, eight hundred pounds of free meat which sold for pennies a pound, was still a way for cowboys to make a living who did not own any eight hundred pound cattle to sell, had no money to buy such cattle with, but who still liked the notion of making a living.

Such as it was.

They had brought three sacks of beans and two sacks of potatoes down into the wild-horse country with them from the nearest town up north, which was Saint George, in Utah, plus some smoking tobacco, salt and whatnot. Now, it was up to the horses.

They spent three days making a trap around the salt-lick. There were no trees worthy of the name, nor close enough anyway, so they wove a faggot fence from dead ocatilla and anything else they could find which was at least six feet tall, and usable for their purpose. Strength would have been desirable, but since wild horses functioned by sight, the important thing with that damned faggot fence was to make it tight enough so that horses could not see beyond it, or through it. That would—usually anyway—prevent a wild stampede through the corral to freedom.

After that, they went back to their top-out to wait. They saw dust banners, usually at a great distance, where horses passed, and three times during their second week on the barranca-top, they saw small bands close enough to make out individual horses. But it was not until near the end of the third week, on a warm night with a two-thirds full moon, that Tom nudged Lew and Reg awake in their bedrolls to excitedly whisper that he had heard animals down in the canyon heading for the salt-lick.

Lew, who was just naturally tender-footed, rolled out, tugged on his boots, grabbed his britches and hurried after Reg and Tom.

They had a good trail down to the west side of the canyon. Tom and Reg made no noise because they were both in their stocking feet. Lew, a few yards farther back, paused to get into his britches. By the time he reached the bottom of the barranca Reg and Tom were hurrying. There was, indeed, a band of animals in the trap noisily and hungrily shoving one another to get at the salt.

There was no gate. It was rarely necessary to build one. But there was a length of rope which could be hauled taut across the opening, and a foul-smelling old stained piece of ground-cloth canvas which was pulled over the rope. A wild horse would batter his head bloody against a post before he would even approach that canvas with the rank man-scent embedded in it.

Tom, whose club foot hindered his speed, was passed by Reg Bentley in their haste to yank up the rope and fling the canvas over it. Lew, who was still a fair distance farther back, caught up with Tom Lee at about the time Reg yanked the rope, lunged to grab the old canvas—and let go with a roar of pain, nearly fell, then with fierce profanity managed to heave the canvas into place.

Inside, the animals fought and snorted and circled in panic. They were trapped.

Reg sat on the ground rocking back and forth and holding his right foot while he groaned. In his hurry, he had hit his stocking foot against a solid round boulder of grey granite. His big toe had taken the brunt of that collision and he was positive the toe was broken.

Lew got up to the gate, ignored his partner's profane lamentations, tried to make out the number of animals they had trapped, and slowly began to scowl and wrinkle his nose as Tom came limping up, grinning from ear to ear.

'We got a band,' the big Mormon exclaimed. 'Look at 'em. Good thing I'm a light sleeper. You fellers would have let 'em fill up and wander off again.'

Lew leaned down. Moonlight helped visibility, but the ruckus inside the corral had stirred up clouds of brown dust. Even so, Lew could make out bald faces. Too many bald faces. Bald faced horses were not unusual, but he'd never before seen an entire band of mustangs, all with bald faces. And he had that rank smell in his face now, stronger than before.

He was turning towards Tom when Reg got up to limp over to the gate. Right at this moment what Reg Bentley needed was anything at all which would convince him breaking his big toe had been in a good cause. The toe was not actually broken, but Reg would not discover that for another couple of hours.

He leaned beside Lew looking in at the milling animals as Lew spoke to Tom Lee. 'Tom, they all got bald faces.'

Lee was still smiling when he peered through the dust without saying anything for a while, and when he spoke he ignored Lew's statement. 'Must be thirty head. That's a big band. Usually there ain't more'n . . .'

'Tom, you damned idiot, those are *cattle*,' Lew exclaimed. 'I can smell 'em. We got someone's damned white-faced cattle in the trap!'

For a moment no one spoke, then Reg straightened up and turned toward the big Mormon, fighting mad. 'You half-wit! You big overgrown *estupido*! You damned . . . I broke

8

my foot to close the gate, you damned Mormon bastard. I got a notion to beat your head in!'

Tom stood like stone as though he had not heard a word. The animals were calming by now, some edged over through the dust to push long faces toward the men at the gate. They were indeed Hereford cattle.

Tom Lee watched Reg turn away, limping badly. He said, 'It sounded like horses. From up yonder I couldn't see them . . . Reg, I'll help you back up the trail.'

Reg turned. 'Don't you come near me. I'll kill you!'

As Lew started back with Reg he said, 'Tom, let 'em out.'

Lee remained behind to loosen the rope and remove the canvas. He remained down in the canyon by himself until the cattle had all left the trap, had turned westerly behind a wicked-horned old dry cow, trooping back toward the lower country. What they wanted now, after licking salt, was water. The old cow would lead them to it.

Tom eventually, and reluctantly, returned to the horse-camp atop the barranca. By then, it was turning cold and dawn was no more than a couple of hours away.

CHAPTER TWO

THE LONG WAIT

The toe was discoloured and twice its normal size but when Lew told Reg to move it, it turned out not to be broken, just badly sprained.

Tom remained over beside the stone ring where they cooked, and although Reg's anger had subsided, his disgust had not. He said, 'Tom, until I can walk again, you're goin' to take my share of the cooking.'

There was no dissent from over by the stone ring. In fact Tom would not even look up and meet Reg's glare. When he and Lew took the horses over to the creek, and filled the canteens while the animals were tanking up, Tom said, 'I didn't do it on purpose, Lew. I had no idea anyone was runnin' cattle down here. They wasn't a couple of years back when I was down here ... Maybe if I gave Reg my silver belt buckle he'd feel better.'

Lew, who had recognised the big Mormon's limitations before the three of them had teamed up to head south after mustangs, and who liked Tom Lee, tried to make it a little easier by saying, 'Naw. Keep the silver buckle. He'll get over it.'

'He was awful mad.'

'Yeah. I've partnered with Reg for a long time. I've seen him get that mad before. It takes a while but he gets over it.'

'Did he ever get that mad at you?'

Lew nodded. 'A few times.'

'Yeah, but he ain't going to be able to do much on that sore foot for a while.'

'Tom, quit worrying about it. Don't talk to him about it. It'll just fire him up again.'

'Well, but I'd like to tell him I'm sorry.'

'Wait. Tell him that when he can walk again ... You got those canteens full? Then let's head back.'

When they returned to camp there were waves of heat out over the endless miles of open country. It was hot atop the barranca too, but almost every afternoon a slight breeze arrived and continued to blow until about sundown.

Reg had plenty of time to clean his guns, occasionally use some of their water to wash his shirt, and most of all, to lie up there watching the land in all directions.

Lew and Tom returned from the canyon one mid-day after chasing off several spooky, slab-sided range cattle, and found Reg over by the juniper tree flat on his belly like a lizard, watching something a long way off. They joined him in the shade and he pointed eastward as he spoke.

'Out by that red-rock bluff. The one with some tall brush at its base ... Watch.'

11

They watched. For a long time they simply hunkered and peered from beneath pulled-forward hatbrims without seeing anything. Then there was movement. It was distant and raised no dust but it definitely was movement, and in a country where any kind of movement relieved the utter, desolate stillness, movement meant a living creature.

Lew settled belly-down as he said, 'I wish I owned a pair of spy-glasses.'

No one commented.

Lew also said, 'If it's horses they're sure taking their time. You reckon there might be a spring at the base of that red bluff? The brush sure looks healthy.'

Tom Lee leaned a moment, then spoke. 'Watch now. There's a buckskin horse comin' out of the brush . . . Watch.'

They watched. Tom was correct. Not only was there a buckskin, but coming out of the brush in single file behind the buckskin were other horses. It was in fact a fair-sized band, and they were relaxed and calm, which was unusual. It did not take much to spook mustangs who only survived at all because they were always prepared to flee at high speed at the slightest hint of peril. Even a light breeze through clumps of grass would start them running.

But these horses were browsing in a westerly direction behind the buckskin as quietly as old broke saddle-stock. Lew's heart-rate increased a

12

little as he watched. The horses were grazing directly toward the low, southerly shoulder of the barranca. Unless they changed course they would graze around toward the rocked-off southern end of the cul-de-sac canyon and would miss the salt—and the trap—entirely. He mopped sweat with a limp sleeve and said, 'We got to get them heading north up around our barranca so's they'll see the open canyon and maybe smell salt.'

The rational answer to that, at least to people who made motion pictures, would be for all three of them to pile onto their horses, ride down off the barranca and somehow or other get behind the wild horses and drive them into the canyon. The brutal truth was different. In the first place in open country there had never been a tame horse bred and broke who could carry a man and a heavy saddle through a hundred and ten degree desert heat in a race with a mustang and win. In the second place wild horses knew all about watching for movement too; at the first, distant sighting of mounted men, they would simply throw up their tails and run belly-down. And they could keep on running in blast-furnace heat long after other horses gave out.

Reg sat up, carefully picked a tick off his arm and said, 'They'll go up-country. That buckskin's following a cow trail.'

He was right, but for another hour Lew and Tom were not convinced he was right, not until they could see the horses well enough to count them. By then it was obvious that the animals were angling slightly northward as they grazed along.

Tom's red face showed pure avarice. 'Fifteen head. That's good wages for the time we been here.'

'They're not in the trap yet,' stated Reg dourly.

Lew glanced up to make a guess about the time of day from the location of the sun. If nothing spooked the horses, if they did not perversely decide to change course, and if they did not stop in some shade out there, somewhere, to doze through the hottest part of the day, they might reach the canyon's mouth by mid or late afternoon. As he looked down again, watching the buckskin, he remembered something a cowman for whom he had worked in Colorado had once told him: In baseball, a man can be struck out three strikes. In the cattle or horse business he's got the weather against him most of the time, prices over which he has absolutely no control, diseases for which he knows no cure, predators he can ride his butt raw trying to keep down, as well as such epidemics as sidehill-abortion. That is five strikes, and it's only part of the damned list.

He counted the horses, accepted Tom's figure of fifteen head, and considered the odds against capturing this band. When he looked up and saw Reg gazing at him, he said, 'You should have listened to your paw and been a stone mason.'

Reg thought about that, fished around for his makings and was manufacturing a cigarette before he replied. 'Stone masons develop bad backs,' he said, and lighted up as he looked past at Tom Lee. 'In this business you only get sprained toes.'

Tom neither opened his mouth nor took his eyes off the oncoming horses.

The heat was heavier down on the flats than it was atop the barranca, and right on schedule the little breeze arrived. They sat in comfort in juniper shade. Ordinarily juniper shade did nothing to inspire a man; junipers smelled like wet diapers, but heat of the variety those horses were walking through was worse.

Reg hobbled back to camp for a canteen, hobbled back and sat down again. The horses were fanning out a little as they moved, seeking clumps of grass amid the stones and ground-cover underbrush. As far as Lew knew, no one had ever bothered to figure it out, but in country like this it probably required at least one hundred acres to maintain one head of livestock. Antelope did well where there was more brush than grass, but antelope were browsing, not grazing critters.

Tom drank, put the canteen aside and fished forth a large blue bandana to mop sweat off

15

with, then he grinned and said, 'There's some decent horses in that band.' He sounded surprised, and had a right to be. Not only did some of the mustangs have fair size to them, but they were in good flesh. 'I'll bet the In'ians never seen that bunch.'

Reg grunted. 'What In'ians?'

Tom did not take his eyes off the horses. 'They're around; south and east of here. Over by Short Creek ... that's a village a long ways off ... there's In'ians in the canyons and around. They'd shoot those horses.'

Reg punched out his cigarette and leaned back against the juniper tree, studying the mustangs. Tom was right, there were a few horses of quality down there. That buckskin for example, looked to be maybe a little over nine hundred pounds in size. A thousand pounds would have been better, but still, the buckskin was large enough to make a saddle animal out of, and from a distance it appeared to be a handsome animal. But then, the prettiest colour in a horse was fat, and all those horses were in good flesh. Springtime was fading before the onslaught of summer, which meant the bunch-grass would cure on the stalk. Grazing animals held their own on dry feed. They did not add any weight, and if they had to move a lot, and move fast, they fell off. But these horses had not yet begun to suffer from that kind of natural attrition. Reg turned toward his partner and

16

said, 'Fifteen head—if we catch 'em—in good condition up at Saint George, ought to bring us how much?'

Lew was careful with his answer. 'How much will the market pay now? We been away a long time.'

'Make a guess.'

'It was two cents a pound the last I heard. Those critters are in good flesh. I got no idea what their average weight will be.'

'The buckskin'll come close to nine hundred,' said Tom Lee. 'So will that bay horse and the black. But there are some runts. Maybe six hundred and fifty average, for the whole band.'

Lew shrugged. 'How about sixty-five dollars for the lot?'

Reg was satisfied, and Tom was more interested in the way the horses were finally beginning to come around the base of the barranca in the general direction of the canyon's mouth.

They drank, then had to move to the north of the juniper in order to have the mustangs in sight. The horses were still making a very leisurely graze, some several yards farther out, none of them hurrying. But, close enough for the men to see them better, two things became obvious. There was no stallion with the band, which meant they were probably all bred mares, and the buckskin, which was evidently the leader, was beginning to raise her head now and then to test the air for scent.

That was invariably a wild horse's first means of self-protection and the sweating wild-horse hunters watched that buckskin like hawks. The entire band was close enough now to see the mouth of the cul-de-sac canyon. If a wind came now, and blew toward the mustangs from within the canyon, it would carry the rank scent of men with it. But there was no wind, and would not be one. Not this time of day, and rarely this time of year.

If the animals entered the canyon and went deep enough into it, they would eventually pick up man-scent from that old canvas ground-cloth beside the trap, but by then they would have only one way back out, and as the men leaned, watching intently, they had the answer to that. They would simply go down their trail and fan out to block the single entrance and exit.

Reg finally arose impatiently to go back where their horses were dozing to begin saddling. Lew went back too, leaving Tom to watch, and if the horses entered the canyon, he was to hasten back and tell them. They would then allow the mustangs time enough to get well into the canyon, and go down the trail on horseback to keep their wild horses in.

Lew had sweat running under his clothes, as much from excitement and anticipation as from the shimmering waves of heat. Far out, finally, the heat looked like a thin layer of smoke the way it obscured distances and softened outlines.

Tom came back, his red face sweat-shiny and showing excitement. 'They're in,' he announced, and went after his horse and outfit. Reg took the lead with Lew following. Neither of them glanced back where Tom was fumbling awkwardly in haste to rig out his horse.

For several minutes after Lew and Reg were down the far side of the barranca where they could watch the buckskin mare leading her band in the direction of the faggot trap at the far lower end of the canyon, the mustangs had no inkling of trouble. They did not look upwards, they looked left and right and dead ahead but not upwards, and they might never have done that if the sound of shod horses crossing rock had not reached them.

They suddenly halted and whirled, poised for immediate flight. Reg urged his mount recklessly down the narrow trail with Lew in his wake. For a moment the wild horses rolled their eyes to find the source of sound. By the time they looked up and finally saw mounted men between them and the mouth of the canyon, it was too late. They were at least three-quarters of a mile down the canyon.

They knew they could not get past in time and stood like statutes until the buckskin mare whirled to lead them in a wild run due southward around the trap.

There was no way out, down there. She

wasted time rushing back and forth, even trying to paw her way up the jumbled stone wall which formed the lower end of the canyon.

Reg and Lew loped toward positions at the canyon's mouth. Tom Lee came a little later. All three men sat their saddles in blazing afternoon heat, watching dust rise down where the trapped animals were running in wild panic seeking a way to escape.

Lew lifted his hat, mopped sweat, re-set the hat and smiled at Reg. 'Got 'em,' he said.

Bentley grinned back. 'So far so good. Now comes the rough part.'

They sat a long time waiting for the first panic to subside down at the lower end of the canyon. It never did entirely subside, but exhaustion made some of the frantic mustangs slacken off in their attempt to claw their way up the stone barrier at the lower end of the canyon, and turn to face the distant mounted men, sweat dripping from belly-hair in steady trickles, eyes bloodshot and nostrils fully distended.

CHAPTER THREE

A NIGHT TO REMEMBER

They sent Tom back to the camp for bedrolls and food. During his absence Reg and Lew dismounted to hunker in the shade of their horses, watching and waiting for most of the dust to settle.

Several horses made feinting runs at the squatting men, who sat watching. When neither mustanger succumbed to the fear the horses intended to inspire, the horses spun and raced back toward the trap.

Lew said, 'Too bad there's no water in the canyon. We could take our time at handling them if there was.'

Reg rolled and lit a smoke, shook off sweat and watched the buckskin mare. After a long while he said, 'I'll take her for part of my share.'

Lew was perfectly agreeable. 'Sure. But she won't be broke by the time we trail them north.'

Reg was silent again for a long time, and looked away only when they heard Tom coming back.

They made a dry camp in the centre of the canyon's mouth, gathered faggots for their little fire, and rolled out their blankets. Lew watched Reg encircle his bedroll with a hair rope, said nothing and stifled a smile. He had been told the same story about snakes and gila monsters and tarantulas refusing to crawl over a hair rope to get near a man sleeping on the ground, and he knew it was a damned lie. He also knew every man had to make certain discoveries for himself.

Tom cooked a pot of beans, fried the spuds, and made a potful of coffee which tasted as bad as original sin. His companions did not complain, although perhaps they should have because, although Tom was a jack-Mormon in most ways, he remained steadfast at least about coffee and did not drink it, which was probably why he couldn't make a decent potful.

They felt relaxed and comfortable after sundown when the direct rays of heat departed, and after they had something behind their belts. Lew and Reg smoked. Tom did not use tobacco, again, less because he was a good Mormon than because he had just never picked up the habit.

He listened to the horses down by the faggot trap and grinned. 'All's we got to do now is earn our wages,' he said. 'It won't take long, them without no water for a few days.'

Lew was dozing with his head cradled against the damp sheep pelt lining of the saddle skirts, which were turned up for his pillow. They smelled powerfully of salt-sweat. There were worse pillows, and Lew Palmer had been smelling horse sweat most of his life.

Shortly after night arrived the sound of horses diminished to little more than a restless, rustling sound of iron-hard bare hooves over abrasive stone at the far end of the canyon.

Lew kicked out of his boots, put his hat over the tops to prevent crawling things from climbing down in during the night, and surprising hell out of him come dawn, pulled one old blanket up and went to sleep.

Reg drank from a canteen, massaged his toe, from which nearly all the swelling had gone, and wiggled it in order to feel the extent of the remaining pain. Across the little fire Tom said, 'I'm sorry. I never meant for you to hit no rock. I'd rather it'd been me, Reg.'

The Canadian continued to wiggle his toe and watch it. Finally he replied, 'I knew better. I knew when we ran down there the damned place was full of rocks.' That was as close as Reg Bentley would ever come to announcing forgiveness.

A little later, as he was arranging his blankets inside the encircling horsehair rope he said, 'We got a lot of cutting and splicing to do tomorrow. I hope there's enough rope.'

Tom answered confidently. 'There is. It don't take but a little to make a pair of hobbles ... I hope they don't break no legs though. It'll cut down on the money we'll get for them if they do.'

Reg grunted and bedded down. Tom sat a while longer by the fire then also sought his blankets. He was one of those individuals who went to sleep immediately, and slept like the dead. There was a rumour that people who could sleep like that had clear consciences. Maybe it was true. Tom Lee was as guileless as a puppy. His mistakes were always honest ones.

There was a moon, and twice in the night the mustangs came stealthily up near the mouth of the canyon. Between the mansmell, the evil glowing red eye of the dying little fire, and the alert saddle-stock of the mustangers, they were frightened off each time. Lew and Reg lay on their backs, eyes open, listening. Confident what would happen but listening anyway. Tom's soft snoring did not miss a beat either time.

The night cooled off a little, tired men slept on warm ground, somewhere an owl hooted, which was unusual, and somewhere else it was answered by another owl. The desert had owls; usually they lived in holes in the ground, perhaps because there were so few trees for them to make dens in. And there were rodents in abundance. But this was summertime, owl mating season was past, therefore there was little reason for owls to be calling back and forth, particularly in the shank of the night which was when they concentrated almost exclusively on skimming on silent wings a few feet above the ground hunting food.

The hobbled horses stirred a little near the sleeping men, gazing intently into the northward night. They were not frightened, they were simply very interested in a scent which was coming down to them.

For a long time there was silence. Eventually, the saddle-stock abandoned their vigil and went back to seeking and picking grass stalks.

There was horse feed enough, but using

horses, unlike mustangs who could eat any time, had to graze when they could.

Finally, the mustangs seemed to settle down. At least there were no more stealthy forays toward the only escape route, and sounds from down behind the trap diminished. Horses shared one distinction with men; they could sustain panic or excitement just so long, then they became tired and required rest.

It was a pleasant late night. Although the rocks and the earth retained a residue of the daylong heat, the air was cool. Tired men slept well, particularly in the later hours. The hobbled saddle horses did not. That familiar scent was stronger now, and they watched intently for the appearance of those who were making it.

They might have nickered when the horsemen appeared like wraiths, riding soundlessly a short distance west of the dry camp. If they had nickered ... but they didn't, and those shadowy apparitions passed by riding down toward the lower end of the blind canyon.

For about fifteen minutes nothing changed. The owls no longer hooted, and the faint little nighttime breeze which had carried the scent of horsemen to the using horses, had died away completely.

The wild horses picked up the approaching scent of mounted men long before the silent riders got near, and typically, they reacted with instant, wild panic. The horsemen were deliberately staying to the west side of the canyon. That left the east side unobstructed, and predictably the terrified mustangs broke away in a wild run toward the mouth of the canyon over in that direction.

Reg struggled up out of a deep and dreamless slumber, aroused by the fury of the oncoming stampede. Instinct told him nothing would stop the wild horses this time. He pushed up and yelled at Lew. The horses were so close by the time Lew and Tom awakened it was possible to hear them grunt with effort as they lunged ahead.

Lew sprang to his feet running. He went westerly. Reg was also on his feet, but his haste was hampered by a limp. Tom Lee, who was not quick-witted at any time, stood up with a blanket falling from his shoulders, looked at the oncoming horses for an agonising moment, then turned and lumbered in the wake of his companions, his club foot making his flight resemble the ungainly lope of a large bear.

The mustangs went over the camp in blind terror, flinging blankets, cooking utensils, even saddles and bridles in all directions. Close up behind them the ghostly riders spurred hard in the rising dust, not visible to Reg, Lew and Tom because of darkness, dust, and the fact that they had no idea the horses were not stampeding on their own.

It was over in moments. Just the horse-scented dust remained. Lew looked around at his companions. Both were standing like stones, gazing up past the mouth of the canyon where the horses were no longer visible, but seemed to be turning eastward in the general direction they had come from before entering the canyon, judging from the sound.

Five minutes later the sound was also gone. Only dust showed that a stampede of wild horses had passed through.

Lew started back toward the camp. Reg limped in his wake and Tom ambled like a sleep-walker.

Their saddles had survived intact, although they had marks which would never disappear. Reg's headstall and bit were uninjured, but evidently his reins had got wrapped around a mustang's leg because the reins were broken and they did not find the bridle until after sunrise. It was a hundred yards away.

Their blankets had been trampled, their cooking implements had been struck repeatedly and dented. Where the little fire had been there was nothing, not even any char. The ground had been churned for several yards to the east and west.

Very little was said as they brought everything together near where the fire had been, then hunted scattered faggots to make another fire with, fill the dented coffee pot from one of the miraculously uninjured canteens, and make some hot coffee.

Dawn was approaching when they finally sat down with the shock gone, replaced by angry exasperation. Whatever else they accomplished on this trip, there was one thing they knew would never be accomplished, those wild horses could not be got anywhere near this canyon again. Probably never in their lives, but certainly not this season.

The sun rose over their barranca. Tom returned from being out where the hobbled saddle animals had tried to flee in their hobbles, sank down upon his old saddle and said, 'The horses didn't get hurt none. Just a little chafing is all. If they'd got loose we'd have been bad off.' Tom picked up his empty tin cup, methodically refilled it, then settled back to speak again. 'That wasn't no free-runnin' stampede.'

Lew and Reg lifted their eyes to the big Mormon's face. Lew said, 'Why wasn't it?'

'Because I seen shod horse marks.'

Lew continued to stare at Tom Lee. 'Where?'

Tom drained his cup and put it aside as he arose. 'I'll show you.'

Sunlight was beginning to chase the last of the shadows along the west side of the canyon, and although the air still smelled of horses, the dust had settled.

Tom quartered a little, then halted like a bird

dog with one big arm extended. 'There,' he exclaimed. 'Ain't just one set neither. Look over here.'

They spent a half hour finding, and examining, the deep impressions of horseshoes in the churned soil. Where those steel shoes had encountered rocks, there were clearly visible stone bruises.

Reg went to a big boulder and leaned against it while he gazed up beyond the mouth of the canyon. Losing the horses bothered him, of course, but something else bothered him just as much. He had been lying atop the barranca for more than a week watching the entire countryside as far as a man could see, and not once had he seen horsemen, buildings, or even the kind of ruts wagons left.

'Where in the hell did they come from?' he eventually asked of no one in particular. 'How did they get in there—right past us?'

Tom gestured. 'Over yonder, east of where we was sleeping. They walked their horses slow. The ground's sort of powdery. They plain rode past us an' got down there. Then run the horses ... We're damned lucky, do you fellers know that? They run the horses right up over our camp. If we hadn't been lucky we'd have got ground into—'

'Tom!' Reg said sharply. 'You said there weren't any people down here.'

'There wasn't. Never have been, except

maybe for the folks over at Short Creek ...
Maybe half a dozen families. They got no reason
to go to all this trouble to get horses. They got
plenty of their own. Anyway, Short Creek
settlement is maybe twenty miles from here,
eastward ... I ain't been down here for a few
years. I told you that, Reg. I told you exactly
how it was the last time. There wasn't
nothing...'

Reg shifted his weight so that it was
supported by his uninjured foot. 'Those cattle
we got in the trap,' he said.

Tom nodded about that, his low forehead
creasing with two deep lines. 'Yeah. There
wasn't any cattle down here either.'

'There are now, Tom.'

'Yeah, I know that. But we never saw any
riders, Reg.'

'There is a camp all the same, Tom. There has
to be.'

'Well, you should have seen it from atop the
barranca. You been lyin' up there ever since you
hurt your foot.'

'I didn't see anything,' exclaimed Bentley,
irritated by Lee's statement. Then he also said,
'A man can't see everything from up there. This
damned country has a lot of bluffs in it, like that
red-rock bluff we saw the mustangs come
around yesterday ... I'll tell you one thing:
Those riders didn't drop from the sky.
Somewhere out there, is a camp.'

Lew had been silent up until now. 'Why?' he asked, then answered himself. 'Because they wanted the horses. All right. And sure as hell they knew where we were and they've been spying on us. Saw us trap the horses in here yesterday, and came after the horses for themselves last night.'

Tom's frown deepened. 'That's horse stealing,' he said, having just made a discovery that aroused his indignation. 'There's laws against that.'

Reg gazed steadily at the large man. 'What law? Where is the law? We're ninety miles from a town where there might be a lawman. There is no law down here, Tom.'

CHAPTER FOUR

A BAD TRIP

They moved their camp to the spring where they had been getting water since arriving in the Wolf Hole country. There did not appear to be any further reason to watch for wild horses atop the barranca, and at the spring there was tree shade and some grass. They also bathed for the first time in a couple of weeks, and although that helped them get through the first day after someone had stampeded their horses, it did not

31

leaven their feelings at all.

The following morning they saddled up, rode back to the canyon's mouth, picked up the trail of the mustangs and followed it until the sun was almost directly overhead, then left the trail to go down into a wide arroyo which may have been a prehistoric watercourse, and off-saddled to rest while their animals hunted grass.

The trail had led them in the direction of that red-rock bluff they had seen yesterday when the mustangs had come around the base of it. It was Lew's innate caution that kept them from pushing on over there. There was no way to see what lay behind the bluff, and although Tom scoffed at the suggestion that there might be a camp around there, Lew chose to be cautious.

Reg's mood was bleak. It had taken him a little time to put it all together and come up with what had obviously been a deliberate attack on their camp, and their trapped horses. Now, he wanted to find the men who had done those things.

They shared a canteen, killed an hour, then struck out again, this time with Lew leading them northward well beyond rifle range, so that when they turned eastward again they would be able to see behind the red-rock bluff.

The heat was almost a physical force each saddle animal had to lean into in order to make progress. The horses would require water before they got back to the base camp. Maybe the wild-horse trail would lead to water.

The trail was easy to follow, and at least during the morning the shod-horse tracks had been not too far in the drag of the mustangs. But by afternoon the mustangs had widened the distance, and by the time Lew halted peering southward down the rear side of the big red-stone cliff, the ridden horses had been greatly out-distanced.

Reg grunted at sight of trees behind the red-rock bluff, where the top-out dwindled down to ground level, its colour changing until, where those trees stood, there was no red colour left.

Reg said, 'That's why the mustangs were over here. Those trees mean water. Let's go.'

Lew and Tom followed as Reg set his horse directly toward the trees. There did not seem to be any reason to exercise additional caution because as far as any of them could see, there was nothing but rock, clumps of grass, those trees, and an azure sky with billowing little fat white clouds overhead. What they watched for was movement, and there was none.

They picked up the shod-horse sign near the base of the bluff where a trail existed, perhaps made by generations of wild horses which had watered over here.

Where the shod-horse marks went over the trail it was not difficult to single them out. There had been four riders.

The trees which sheltered a little sump-spring

cast welcome shade, and the horsemen they were seeking had halted here last night, possibly to tank up their animals, possibly to listen for pursuit.

The mustangs had passed through in the night but had not halted. From this point on there would be no shod-horse tracks within miles of the mustangs.

As they swung off to let their horses drink and pick grass Lew walked out and around, studying the ground. When he had a direction fixed in his mind he returned to the shade and told his companions the horsethieves had gone due south, the wild horses had gone due east. And that seemed to Lew to mean that whoever the horsethieves were, they had not intended to keep the horses, only to liberate them, and that irritated Reg Bentley all over again.

In disgust he said, 'What in the hell is the sense of stealing someone's animals if a man don't expect to keep them.'

They remained on the trail of the horsethieves for two hours of solid riding, and the tracks never deviated. Whoever those men had been, they had had a definite destination after stampeding the mustangs, and they had made no attempt to disguise their sign, or hide it.

Tom was up front on his big roan horse heading for a slow-rising landswell dead ahead when Reg turned to his partner and said, 'They got to know we'll be tracking them.' Reg then lifted his face and turned his head from side to side as though expecting to see someone perhaps sitting a horse in the distance, watching.

Lew had considered this possibility long ago. He had been watching too, but as long as they remained away from big stands of rocks, it was not very likely that someone could ambush them.

He looked ahead, saw Tom halt atop the long-spending rise of land, and waited for Tom to either push on down the far side, or turn back. Instead of doing either, Tom dismounted up there and stood at the head of his horse looking down the slope where neither Reg nor Lew could see.

They surprised a short, fat rattlesnake with a greenish cast to his body. The horses sucked sideways and the rattler did not try to coil, he instead moved as fast as he could toward a dusty big old flourishing bush where there was shade. While he moved ahead his body seemed to move sideways.

They bypassed him and started up the gradual long slope of the landswell. When they were near the top Tom turned and watched their approach.

When they were close Lew raised his voice. 'What's down there, Tom?'

Instead of replying the big man simply stood up there staring at them. Reg was beginning to scowl. He too was aware of Tom Lee's mental

35

limitations but he understood him less than Lew did, and as Lew started to haul back on his reins in response to an instinctive warning, Reg said, 'Big dumb damned fool.'

He barely completed the remark when two men on foot stepped around on each side of Tom Lee, one in plain sight, the other one partially hidden by Tom's horse. Both men had carbines in their hands held low.

Reg grunted in surprise. Lew's horse had stopped. He continued to check up the reins as the partially hidden man called out. 'Ride on up. Keep both hands in sight.'

Lew heard his partner mutter something under his breath as they resumed riding. When they were close enough to make out the bronzed, leathery, hard faces of the two strangers, Tom plaintively said, 'They was lyin' on their bellies and I didn't see 'em until I got right up here.'

One of the men said, 'Shut up,' to Tom, then he gestured with his carbine toward Lew and Reg. 'Get down. Keep your hands in plain sight.'

They swung off, eyed the strangers, and waited for whatever came next. It was not a very long wait. The man who had spoken was young. His companion, who had been partially hidden by Tom's horse, was older. When he moved away from the horse into plain sight he proved to also be larger, rawboned, leathery, greying at the temples, and with a face which seemed to have been blasted out of an environment which was rarely mild. He was a big-boned, slab-sided individual with perpetually narrowed eyes and a bloodless bear-trap mouth. He took his time, studied Lew and Reg, studied their outfits and horses, then grounded his Winchester and leaned on it as he spoke.

'You got not business down here ... Who are you?'

They told him their names.

He continued to study them for a moment before speaking again. 'Wild-horse hunters?'

Lew replied, 'Yes. Until last night anyway.'

The greying man's eyes were barely visible in their creases. 'Not in this country you ain't,' he told them.

Tom Lee, who was as tall as the greying man, and considerably heavier, said, 'Why not, mister? This here has been wild-horse country ever since I can remember.'

The greying man turned and waited a moment before replying, which seemed to be a characteristic of his. 'No more it ain't,' he said a trifle sharply, as though he either did not like being argued with, or was tiring of this meeting. He faced Reg and Lew before speaking again. 'You know the worst thing that can happen to a man down here? Being set on foot. Waterholes are far between, an' between here and Saint George there is a twenty-mile stretch where there ain't no water at all.'

Again, the greying man stared and said nothing over a long interval. Lew used this silence to ask a question. 'What's been bothering me, mister, is why you turned down in this direction once you stampeded our horses. You could have aimed them southward, down here for example.'

The slitted eyes fixed themselves upon Lew Palmer. 'You look like the kind that wonders about things, cowboy ... Those weren't your horses. You understand that?'

The greying man looking steadily at Lew made no move to raise his Winchester, but the rawboned younger man who had been silent thus far, eased back the hammer of his saddlegun without taking his eyes off Lew and Reg, and that was evidently his way of making a point without having to speak to do it.

Lew did not reply, Reg did. 'Wild horses belong to anyone who can catch them,' he exclaimed, ignoring the younger man with the cocked Winchester.

Lew interrupted because he was certain what his partner was going to say next, something about men who stampeded other people's caught horses were thieves, and from the looks of that older man, and his gun-handy friend, Lew had a bad feeling that if Reg made a remark like that, someone was going to get hurt.

He said, 'You didn't keep the horses, mister.'

38

'Don't need them or want them,' retorted the greying man, switching his attention back to Lew Palmer. 'Now you listen to me—all three of you: Turn your horses around, go back the way you came, and after you've struck camp, don't even wait until tomorrow, just point north and keep riding until you got the Saint George rooftops in sight . . . And don't you never come back down here.'

Again, there was one of those long pauses before the greying man finished what he wanted to say. 'If you ain't on your way out of the country tomorrow, we're goin' to take you down here another fifty miles, take your outfits and leave you on foot . . . Well?'

Reg was looking steadily at the greying man, his square jaw set like iron. Lew nudged him, gathered both reins and stepped across his animal. 'Get up there,' he said quietly. Reg and the greying man regarded one another for a moment longer, then Reg did as Lew had said. Tom Lee was the last man to mount up. He looked sideways at the man with the cocked carbine, then walked his horse slowly down where his friends were.

Without a word Lew led the way back over their trail, did not stop for a mile and did not look over his shoulder for at least that long. When they had broken country between themselves and that gradual slope, he turned and looked back. Neither of the armed men were in sight, nor had he expected them to be.

Reg growled, 'I'd like to catch that son of a bitch when his hands are empty.'

Tom plaintively repeated what he had told them earlier. 'I didn't mean to lead you fellers into a trap like that. But when I come up there, they rose up out of the grass and boulders with their guns aimed at me. They'd seen us and told me to get down and stand still and wouldn't nobody be hurt. So I obeyed.'

Lew drank and offered the canteen to Reg. As his partner was drinking Lew studied the countryside. When Reg passed the canteen to Tom, Lew said, 'What bothers me is that there were four of them last night, but only two just now ... I think I know how we can get back around that landswell without hair-trigger and squinty-eyes seeing us, but I'd sure like to know where the other two are.'

'Let's go anyway,' Reg exclaimed, glaring back in the direction of the landswell.

Lew wagged his head. 'Look at this country. If you were afoot down here, with your bad foot and all ... Naw, let's head for camp.'

As Lew turned and started riding, Tom wiped his chin with a soiled sleeve, then said, 'How do you like that?' He was pointing at the ground. Lew and Reg looked down, saw nothing of interest, and as Reg began to scowl, Tom smiled at him. 'Two sets of shod-tracks riding right over our tracks. How do you like

40

that? Them other two was shagging us all the time.'

Lew studied the tracks. So did Reg. But neither of them had the talent for reading sign the big Mormon had. One thing they had learned about Tom Lee was that he was never wrong about what he saw, and that of course resolved any ideas Lew had of stealthily sneaking around that landswell and doing some exploring down the far side.

Reg rode in dogged silence peering into every shadow, at every jumble of boulders, and at every other place two mounted men might be. He did not see anything and neither did his companions.

'Worse than darned In'ians,' Reg muttered. 'Who is that old devil anyway? Why should he care whether we catch a few horses? Tom, did you ever hear that anyone owns this country down here?'

That amused the big Mormon. 'Owns it? Now why would anyone want to own anything like this?'

They had shadows on their left when Lew finally looped both reins, rolled and lit a quirley, then trickled bluish smoke as he gazed at his partner. 'If they just wanted us out of the country, why in hell didn't they ride in last night, or any time last week, and tell us so? Why wait until we had the horses, then go to all the bother of sneakin' in during the night and running off the horses to get us to shag after them—and get caught at it?'

Reg wagged his head. Mysteries did nothing for him.

Lew finished his smoke and killed it on the saddlehorn before speaking again. 'There is almost a full moon tonight,' he said, looking from Reg to Tom Lee, and smiling.

CHAPTER FIVE

CAUGHT!

They ate and rested, talked a little until the sun had been gone a couple of hours, and their horses were rested, then saddled up and started back down there again, but this time they scouted carefully ahead, avoided as much rock as possible so as to minimise the noise, and when they finally had the landswell in sight, with a big old rusty moon soaring above, Lew took the lead and rode eastward until they reached an area where the landswell petered out, the land was flat, and for some reason, there were very few big rocks.

Beyond, as far as they could see anyway, there was more of the same kind of country; rough, rocky, with an occasional stone bluff, a few scattered, under-sized trees, and plenty of buckbrush amid openings where bunch grass grew stirrup-tall.

Tom swung off and sank to one knee looking ahead. Reg and Lew remained in the saddle, ready to push ahead. Tom said, 'That's sure big country down there. Looks like it never ends.'

Reg grunted. 'Get astride and let's go, Tom.'

The large man dutifully arose and went along the left side of his horse as he said, 'We better be real careful because those men are most likely over where that little light is.'

Lew and Reg glanced at Tom as he swung up, then turned to look for a light. Tom raised an arm. 'West an' south. Mostly south. There's maybe a big bluff down there. Anyway, the light's being reflected off something. You see it now?'

They saw it. It was no more than a pinprick of brilliance which ordinarily would have been overlooked it was so small, except that, as Tom had said, it was bouncing off something nearby and behind it. Maybe a rock cliff-face.

Tom rested both hands atop his saddlehorn gazing down there. In a mildly complaining tone he said, 'There's nothin' down there. Why in the hell does anyone want to camp down there? I don't think there's even any water down there.'

Lew asked a question without looking away from the tiny, distant glow. 'You know that country, Tom?'

'Yeah. Well, I used to know it. I an' another

feller shagged some antelope down there one time years back. It's full of big boulders and ticks and . . . Say, maybe that's a cow-camp. Maybe those fellers own them cattle that got caught in our trap.'

Lew was pondering. 'Cowmen aren't that dead set against mustangers.'

Reg was ready to ride. As he lifted his rein-hand he said, 'Let's go get some answers . . . Tom, you got bullets in that carbine?' He started riding towards the far-away pinprick of light without waiting for an answer.

The night was pleasantly cool, and although visibility was limited, it was more than adequate for horsemen to pick their way, even when they eventually got down where the light was more noticeable, and large, round rocks began to litter the area.

Nothing was said for more than an hour. Lew was satisfied that the camp with the light was indeed at the base of a bluff. Beyond that, his mind was full of questions for which he could not even imagine any answers, unless of course those were indeed cattlemen down there.

He did not believe they were. Lew had done his share of range-riding in a lot of different places, and he had never encountered stockmen carrying Winchesters before, who refused to allow him to move through their country.

But what else those men might be, he had no idea. Neither did his companions. Tom

44

persisted in saying they owned the cattle which had been encountered down here, and Reg made no attempt to classify the men. But he was not inclined to view them as friends, and for that reason when they were far enough along to stop in a wide place with two gnarled old trees nearby, Reg said, 'Maybe they're renegades. If they are, maybe they have a man out here somewhere, listening and looking.' He pointed to the old trees. 'It's no more'n a mile and a half from here, on foot.'

The horses were left tied, each mustanger took along his saddlegun and, with Reg leading, they started walking. Avoiding the nigger-head rocks was not difficult, and each stand of buck-brush they encountered offered cover if they wanted to halt, which they occasionally did as they got closer.

The light was not being made by a supper fire, which they had assumed would be the case. It was too unwaveringly steady, and it was too white. Lew thought it was probably a coal oil lamp.

Also, the lamp was not on the ground. If it had been, by the time they were fairly close, it would have been possible to see human silhouettes by lampglow.

Tom reached to touch Reg and as the limping man halted, Tom said, 'Somethin' is wrong over there. We rode all over the country before we made our camp near the blind canyon, and I

45

never saw no wagon tracks.'

Reg scowled.

'That there lantern is settin' on the tailgate of a wagon, Reg, an' there wasn't any sign of a wheeled vehicle coming down from up north. We rode all over that country.' Tom looked troubled. 'How'd they get out here with a wagon?'

Reg accepted the fact that there was a wagon over yonder without being the least interested at this point, as to how it had got there.

He eyed Lew Palmer a trifle quizzically, but Lew was concentrating on what he could make out and had nothing to say until he thought they had wasted enough time, and then he only jerked his head for Reg to start out again.

Reg flung an arm back, halted, and crouched for a moment peering ahead. Lew and Tom sprung their knees too but they did not see whatever it was that had caused a reaction in their companion.

Slowly, Reg started backing. Very slowly and with his eyes fixed on something in front which his friends could not see. All three of them retreated a step at a time, and when Tom Lee's curiosity had about got the best of him, the question he would have asked was answered when a dog began to bark furiously, and moments later someone either tossed a bucket over the lantern or blew it out.

The dog was tethered to a wagon-wheel,

which was fortunate otherwise he would have led the men sitting by the wagon out where Tom, Reg and Lee were back-tracking, and moving a little faster the farther away they got.

But it was not far enough. Even if they had turned and raced for their mounts they could not have closed the distance in time. Behind them, men on horseback were coming in a lope, and someone had freed the dog. He was well ahead of the horses and saw the three fleeing wraiths in the moonlight.

He immediately increased the frenzy of his barking, then ran at Reg, whose sore foot had made it impossible for him to stay up with Tom and Lew.

Reg swore. That, more than the wildly excited dog, stopped Lew and Tom and turned them back. They could see Reg trying to position his carbine so that he could use it as a club if the dog attacked him.

The dog did not attack. Maybe he had been trained not to, and possibly he had done this before and knew that if he simply stood out there snarling and holding the stranger in front of him, his owner would arrive and assume command.

The dog may not have been that intelligent, but as Reg started to turn and the dog lunged and snarled to force him back around, Lew heard the riders. They were riding fanned out and holding a sort of skirmish line as they advanced around stands of brush and large boulders. Lew ran back, elbowed his partner away from the dog and told him to run for it. Reg refused in a blistering retort.

Tom, who had not come ahead, was standing near a large mesquite bush when the horsemen arrived, guns in hand and fanned out. Tom melted from sight in mesquite which had limbs as sharp as arrowheads.

Reg and Lew saw the riders the moment they emerged from the near distance, and Reg started to raise his carbine. Without much doubt he could have shot one man, perhaps two men, but that still left two more, so Lew threw out his arm to force the Winchester down.

They were standing like that when the same slit-eyed, greying man they had encountered before, pushed ahead of his companions and halted twenty feet from the men on foot, and sat there like a Buddha, just chewing his cud of tobacco and staring.

When the other riders converged, there was a total of four men, heavily armed, riding very good horses, and looking as though mercy was something they had never heard of.

The greying man gazed down and said, 'You boys made one hell of a mistake. I offered you a chance.' He spat, looked at the men sitting their horses with him, and gestured. 'Those are the mustangers Sam and I told you about.'

One of the riders scowled. 'You told us there

was three of them.'

As though on cue, someone back in the underbrush cocked a carbine. He did not speak nor move. Neither did the mounted men as they looked in the direction of that little sound.

They waited. Lew visualised Tom Lee hunkering out of sight, not knowing what to do next, unless it was to shoot someone and if he did that all hell would bust loose, so Lew took the initiative. 'Get off your horses,' he said, searching for what to say next as the mounted men stepped down. Reg Bentley growled the next order.

'Get rid of your guns!'

Three of the men looked at the narrow-eyed older man as though expecting guidance. He gave it; without a word he opened his hand and let the gun drop. The other three men did likewise. All four of them were alternately staring toward the underbrush and at Lew and Reg. It was Lew Palmer who now said, 'Move away from the horses.'

Again they obeyed. When they stopped about fifteen feet from the animals Lew picked up some pebbles and threw them. The horses flinched, then turned and trotted back in the direction of the camp, heads up, reins dragging.

Reg went over to gather up the sixguns, which he emptied one by one, flung the bullets in one direction and the guns in another direction, then he stood belligerently glaring at the disarmed foursome. The unarmed men gazed back as still and silent as statues.

Lew let his breath out slowly. His most earnest desire right now was to leave, to return to their north-country horse camp as swiftly as possible. But Reg had another idea. He limped over to stand in front of the rawboned older man, who was taller by half a head, and asked a blunt question.

'Who the hell do you think you are?'

The greying man answered quietly. 'The same man I was yesterday when I gave you fellers some of the best advice you'll ever get. And I'll give it to you again: Get the hell away from here and don't come back. Cowboy, this don't mean anything. You got the drop, but take my word for it, nothing is changed. Just head out of the country, and stay out.'

Reg did not like that any more now than he had liked it earlier, in daylight. He made a little gesture. 'Turn around, mister. We're goin' back to your camp.'

Lew was scowling. He had a premonition. 'Reg . . . !'

Without looking around Bentley said, 'Naw; let's see what they're up to, Lew. Turn around, mister, and walk!'

The older man obeyed without another word. His companions also turned back, and Lew felt like swearing as he too headed toward the camp. Once, he looked back. Tom was coming out of the underbrush clutching his Winchester. Lew thought that every now and then Tom did something surprisingly well. He had done it now, when he had got the drop on the strangers, but as Tom came up behind him, Lew thought that Reg had ruined their chance to get clear of those men without trouble. He did not like the quiet, stony-faced way that older man had agreed to everything. The older man, in Lew's opinion, was one of those calculating and deadly, cold-blooded individuals who anticipated things, and as he walked toward the camp behind Reg and the unarmed strangers, his anxiety increased.

Tom had been correct. They not only had a light wagon with ash bows and a soiled canvas top, but they also had picked their campsite well. A rope corral on three sides held some saddle-stock with their backs to a stone bluff which formed the fourth side of the pen.

There was a dead fire with a coffeepot on some nearby rocks, and when Tom lifted the bucket and lantern-light cast a white glow outward and around, Lew saw that this camp was well provisioned, and had been here for some time. Perhaps for months.

There was even a water cask with a wooden top. Where they hauled the water from to keep the barrel full he had no idea, and right now, as they stood around watching one another, he did not especially care.

Reg was using his handgun to gesture with when he ordered the four strangers to sit down. They obeyed, their interest on Tom Lee, the invisible mustanger who was still clutching his Winchester.

Reg went up to the older man and said, 'What's your name?'

Without hesitation the older man lied quietly, 'Bill Smith.'

Reg did not even scoff. 'All right, Mister Smith—you're not after wild horses. What are you after down here?'

Bill Smith had his answer ready for that question also. 'I've got cattle down here. Four hundred head. It's freegraze country for a hundred miles in all directions.'

Lew would have accepted that. They had encountered cattle. The dog came over and stood looking up at Lew, wagging his tail. Lew leaned and lightly touched the animal's head, then one of the seated men spoke sharply to the dog. 'Rufe, you get over here!'

The dog tucked his tail and immediately moved away from Lee. Reg turned to the dog's owner. 'What's your name?'

'Sam.'

'Sam what?'

'Just Sam. What difference does it make anyway?'

Sam was the younger man who had cocked his carbine when he and Bill Smith had caught

52

Tom, Lew and Reg in the ambush hours earlier, and Reg remembered him for that.

Reg then said, 'Sam, let's you and me go look inside the wagon.'

Lew's impatience and irritation had just about reached their limits. He was about to speak when Sam started to arise from the ground as he was speaking.

'There's nothin' in the wagon but grub and camp stuff, and I think this has gone on about long enough. I am not goin' over there with you. Who the hell do you think *you* are? All we done was go out there a while back to see what was out there. We sure as hell had a right to do that. You're actin' like you're the law and we're some kind of thieves or something.'

Sam and Reg were about the same size, age and heft. They also appeared to have nearly the same disposition. Every eye was on them through the silent, short interval after Sam had spoken and Reg cocked the sixgun in his hand, which was less than ten feet from Sam's belt buckle. They looked steadily at each other and Lew began to have a sinking sensation. He did not see even a hint of capitulation in Sam's face, and unless Sam did decide to obey, he would have put Reg in the position of having to either back down or pull the trigger. Lew knew his partner better than anyone else. He said, 'Sit down, Sam,' and walked up closer. Sam turned slightly to face him, and Lew's left hand shot out with a blur of speed. Sam went down. One of the other men leaned as though to jump up and Reg pointed the cocked Colt directly at the man's face. He very slowly eased back.

Not a word was spoken. Lew motioned for Tom to come closer, then he said, 'Watch them,' and stepped past Bill Smith on his way over to the wagon where the lantern was brightly burning on the tailgate.

CHAPTER SIX

A BUSTED FLUSH

Sam had been telling the truth. Inside, the wagon had crates of tinned food, extra lariats and hobbles, extra blankets, boxes of ammunition for handguns and saddleguns, as well as a box with metal corners and a lock on the hasp which had the word 'Medicine' painted on it.

There were two large wooden crates, also with locks on them, and piled over those big boxes were spare cooking pots and pans, and even two rounds of pitch wood for cutting slivers off to start fires with.

A wooden barrel which held horseshoes was beside a blacksmith's shoeing box with all the appropriate tools in it, plus two boxes of shoeing nails; two different sizes of nails. The box Lew opened held number four, city head, nails. He put the box aside and noticed that one of the big brass locks which secured the nearest of those two large crates was hooked through the hasp but someone had neglected to snap it closed. He shoved aside pots and blankets to get at the big crate, removed the lock and had to strain to lift the lid. The entire big box was massively made, steel reinforced, and very heavy.

Lew looked in. Stood a long time without moving, then gently eased the lid down, stepped back for the lantern, and with it held high, raised the lid again. This time he stood even longer, and when he eventually eased the lid down and turned, holding the lantern, his face was as expressionless as a man's face usually was when he was stunned.

Outside, it was quiet except when someone asked someone else to pass him a canteen and, distantly, a horse blew its nose.

Lew climbed back down out of the wagon, replaced the lantern on the tailgate and without meeting four sets of eyes which were fixed upon him, looked straight out where Reg was standing.

In a very soft voice he said, 'They got two big boxes in there nearly full of gold and silver stuff. I never saw anything like that before in my life.'

Reg said, 'What kind of stuff?'

'Looks like church stuff. Big gold cups and

crucifixes, candlesticks that must weigh thirty pounds. A lot of staffs and other things with jewels inlaid in them ... Go look. I'll watch them for you.' When Reg frowned and hesitated, Lew walked over, drew his handgun and turned facing the seated men who were staring up at him. 'Go look, Reg.'

Bentley limped away and Lew watched until Reg had taken the lantern inside with him, then Lew gazed at the four seated captives. They looked back from blank faces. Lew said, 'Mister Smith ... where in hell did you get all that stuff?'

Smith did not answer. He was slowly skiving a sliver of chewing tobacco off a molasses-hardened plug and did not even lift his face. But when he had the cud settled inside against one cheek, he replaced the plug in a shirt pocket and sat there looking up, with the wicked-bladed knife still in his right hand.

'You should have gone,' he said quietly, then paused for a long time before saying anything else. Bill Smith, or whatever his name was, did not seem to have a nerve in his body. He spat aside, then spoke again. 'You'll never go now.'

They heard Reg's exclamation of profane surprise from inside the wagon. Lew instinctively raised his eyes, and nearby Tom, who had not been as astonished at the discovery of the wagon's contents as Lew had been, turned his carbine toward Bill Smith. He was

56

holding it low in both hands, and now he cocked it.

Lew's eyes sprang back to Smith. The wicked-bladed knife was aimed in his direction and lying lightly poised upon Smith's right hand.

Tom said, 'Throw that thing away, Mister Smith.' He did not sound very menacing, but the Winchester he was holding, cocked and aimed, was menacing.

Bill Smith tossed the knife to one side, then spat again and looked away in bitter disgust. He too, had made an assessment of Tom Lee, the big, ox-eyed Mormon. And as others had been doing for years, he had under-estimated Tom, who for a fact did not look intelligent, and in fact was not intelligent, but he was not a simpleton either, although at times he came close to looking and acting like one.

Reg climbed gingerly down from the wagon and walked slowly back where he cast just one glance at his partner, then faced the greying, older man whose jaws were methodically working on the cud of tobacco.

'Where did that stuff come from?' Reg asked. 'It's religious stuff. It didn't come from just one church, there's too much of it.'

Bill Smith chewed, eyed Reg, and when it did not seem that he would open his mouth, he finally spoke. 'It's legal. That's all you got to know.'

Reg looked slowly from Smith to each of Smith's companions, one at a time, and finally stepped over in front of a thin, tall man with a wedge-shaped face and a prominent adam's apple. They gazed at one another a long time before Reg leaned, caught cloth and lifted the thin man to his feet. With their faces inches apart Reg said, 'Talk! Start talkin' and don't stop until I tell you to.' He drew his sixgun, cocked it and pushed it into the soft belly of the tall, thin man.

Reg did not utter another word. The silence ran on until it seemed unable to last any longer, then Reg released his hold and stepped back, tipping the gun barrel as he was moving.

'We trade for it,' the thin man burst out, running the words together. 'Ain't nothin' illegal about how we . . .'

'Who do you trade with?'

'They are Messicans.'

Reg's brows dropped. They were a long way from the border between Mexico and Arizona. 'Mexicans rob churches in Arizona and sell you that stuff?'

'No . . . Well, I never asked where it come from. They just ride in an' trade an' ride away.'

Lew who had been watching the tall, thin man closely, interrupted to make a statement. 'You're holding back,' he said and started moving toward the thin man. Reg waited until Lew was almost in front of the tall man, then

58

moved slightly to one side, and said, 'Start with his right arm. Break it at the elbow. They heal up stiff. Then the left arm and . . .'

'He told you the truth,' Bill Smith said, starting to stand up. 'We been trading with Messicans down here for about a year now. As far as we know, it's plumb legal and all. And besides, Slim don't know any more than he just told you.'

Lew and Reg both looked at Smith. Lew said, 'Where do they get that stuff?'

Smith went into one of his periods of hanging-fire before replying. 'We buy—that's all I can say.' The perpetually narrowed eyes studied Lew and Reg as though to guess if this would be enough, and of course it wasn't, so he added a little more. 'We camp here, and they ride in. Sometimes it's a month, sometimes a couple of months. Meanwhile we run some cattle.'

That did not answer the question, so Lew tried again, in a roundabout way. 'How long you been down here, with the cattle?'

Bill Smith hung-fire again, expectorated, glanced at his companions, who were watching him, then answered. 'We trailed in a month back.'

'From where?'

'South.'

'With the wagon?'

'Yes. We scouted up the country couple of years back and found a way to bring in the wagon.'

Lew nodded. So much for how they had got here without leaving tracks from up north, where the only road existed. What Smith had said could be done. It would not be easy and it would require time, but a wagon could get in here, if someone had enough reason and resolve to want to bring one in. Now, he went back to his original theme. 'You've been in this business a couple of years then. Maybe a little less. Mister, you're not the kind of a man who just sets up an isolated camp, using cattle to make everything look normal, and buys gold objects with jewels all over them from Mexicans without knowing where that stuff comes from.'

When Lew stopped speaking and stood looking at the older man, Bill Smith spat, considered the empty land beyond reach of the lantern, and finally said, 'They're building up a big arms cache for a revolution in Messico. It takes money, and it takes time.'

'This stuff comes from Mexico?' Lew asked, and the older man slowly nodded his head. He was answering questions without seeming to be holding much back, and normally Lew would have been made suspicious about that, but right now he was only interested in those big chests full of enormously valuable gold, silver, and jewelled objects. He had made no real attempt to guess their value, although when he had been in the wagon it had occurred to him that what he was staring at was quite likely worth more money than he could imagine, let alone count.

Bill Smith said, 'The wild horses ... We had 'em trapped once and broke a big black, a buckskin mare and a sorrel to pack. They got loose one night. Slim, there, saw the smoke when you fellers set up camp on the barranca. We got atop the bluff at the lower end of the blind canyon and watched you boys make that trap ... If the damned horses hadn't gone in there, we'd have left you alone, but you caught the animals we figured to use. So we had to turn 'em loose.'

The younger man named Sam interrupted to ask garrulously if he could stir up a fire and put the coffeepot on to boil. Reg nodded, and watched Sam move closer to the fire ring and go to work.

Bill Smith stood gazing out into the ghostly night where moonlight bathed the countryside in an almost eerie, soft brilliance.

One of the unarmed men had sat in silence throughout all that had happened up to this point. He was darkly bearded, had black eyes, a mahogany-coloured hide, and thick, curly hair which badly needed trimming. He was not very tall but he was massively put together, and obviously very strong. He was leaning against an upended saddle gazing sardonically, and fearlessly, at his captors. When Sam went to the fire-ring, the dark man lifted his battered and stained old hat, scratched vigorously for a moment, lowered the hat and looked directly at Reg, whom he had evidently singled out among his captors as the most belligerent. He said, 'You're a damned fool, cowboy.'

Reg was bristling as he turned. The dark man's gaze did not waver. He almost seemed amused. 'If you wasn't a damned fool, you'd have done as you was told, an' if you'd done that, you'd have still been alive tomorrow. You and your partners.'

Reg holstered his sixgun and moved over in front of the lounging, dark man. 'Care to bet money we won't be alive tomorrow?' he said.

The dark man's amused look deepened slightly. 'No, because I don't like sure bets... Cowboy, look behind you.'

Lew felt the cold chill before either of his companions felt it. Reg, scoffing at what he considered the oldest trick in the world, growled something which Lew did not hear because he was turning.

It looked like a small army. They were standing out there upon the fringe of the lighted area, with guns in their hands. Behind them, more men were holding horses. They were Mexicans, stained, faded, venomous looking, and clearly very good at what they had just accomplished—stalking the camp without a sound because they had seen three men with weapons holding Bill Smith and his riders prisoner in their own camp.

Quietly, Lew interrupted Reg to say, 'Turn around.'

Tom obeyed when Reg did. Tom's mouth dropped open. He was speechless with surprise. So was Reg, but only briefly, then, with comprehension coming, he swore.

Bill Smith stood hip-shot, close to smiling. He had been awaiting the arrival of these men tonight, and he had deliberately made revelations in order to keep the conversation going, while at the same time he watched the outer limits of the camp. It had worked surprisingly well.

Now, without moving or losing his small smile he addressed the mustangers in his quiet, drawling voice. 'It's up to you, gents, but there's fifteen of 'em out there, and what you're lookin' at is not all of them. There are others around. I'd as soon you'd make a fight of it. That'd solve things for me. But it's up to you.'

The dark, powerfully-built man remained in his lounging position on the ground as he called quietly in Spanish to the motionless Mexicans. One of them showed even white teeth when he laughed and called back. Then he cocked and aimed his sixgun, and the men with him took their cue from this and did likewise.

CHAPTER SEVEN

CONDEMNED MEN

Sam walked over from the fire-ring and from the rear hit Lew as hard as he could. Lew went down with dust spurting where he landed.

Finally, that dark, powerful man got to his feet, dusted off his britches, and went over to Reg with his hand extended. 'The gun,' he said and Reg, who was looking from Lew, who was unconscious a yard away, to the man who had struck him, did not face around quickly enough. The dark man's smile blinked out, his extended hand rolled into a fist, and he lunged, striking Reg once over the heart and again along the slant of the jaw. Reg went backwards, rolled once and lay stone-still on his face, and the dark man leaned to lift away Reg's holstered Colt. He cocked it, grinning again, pointing the sixgun at Tom Lee, but Bill Smith snapped at him curtly, 'Forget that for now. We got work to do.' Smith called in Spanish to the Mexicans. One lean, fairly tall man came forward, dark eyes going from the two unconscious men on the ground to big Tom Lee, whose carbine and sixgun were yanked away by the thin man called Slim.

Bill Smith started to speak in fluent Spanish, and now he did not hesitate between sentences.

When he finished the lean Mexican turned and almost casually sang out an order to the other Mexicans.

There were twenty of them, all stained from travel and from living for a long period of time in the same clothing, but the pack mules they led into the light were handsome, strong animals in good flesh. Each mule was carrying an empty pack rig with slack britchings and breast collars. The Mexicans began removing the pack outfits, and hobbling the mules. While this was in progress Bill Smith and the lean Mexican stood in casual conversation drinking hot coffee. No one paid any attention to the unconscious men, but a squatty, ape-like dark Mexican *arriero* went over beside Tom and grinned upwards as he said something in Spanish, which Tom did not understand, but he smiled back, and the Mexican threw back his head and roared with laughter to find that the *norteamericano* had thought it amusing that the *arriero* had called him a *puerco pendejo*.

Bill Smith accepted a heavy pouch with leather-reinforced corners and top-strap where a brass padlock held the pouch closed, and stood hefting it while he gazed at the lean Mexican. Smith was not smiling. The Mexican, reading Smith's expression correctly, made a gesture of indifference and spoke in English.

'It was too late to stop them. But it won't make any difference. They killed the guard and driver and dumped the stagecoach down into an arroyo . . . You have the payroll.'

Smith replied in the same language. 'The agreement was that you wouldn't do anything like that north of the border.'

The Mexican remained unperturbed, even in the face of Bill Smith's obvious, and cold, disapproval. 'It was a hundred miles from here. Maybe a hundred and fifty miles . . . Do you have the cache?'

Smith hung fire, looking steadily at the Mexican, before nodding as he tossed down the money-filled pouch and turned to lead the way over toward the corralled horses at the base of the bluff.

Two villainous Mexicans sauntered over where Tom Lee was standing, and looked him up and down, then one of them leaned a little. When he straightened up he was holding a large knife in his right fist, and he was grinning. The other Mexican was lean with a face that glistened with sweat in the lamp-light. He seemed to be ordering words before uttering them, and when he finally spoke, he said, '*Vaquero*, this is Manuel. He hasn't killed a *gringo* in three months. Do you want to fight him?' The lean man drew a large knife from its sheath and held it out, grip first, toward Tom.

Tom looked from the proffered knife to the Mexican named Manuel, whose close-set dark eyes with their muddy whites were fixed upon

66

him. Manuel was a killer.

From beyond the fire-ring that dark man who had knocked Reg senseless spoke curtly in English. 'You go with the others to the cache and put that knife away or I'll make you eat it.'

Manuel turned and smiled. He did not understand English and thought he was being encouraged, but his lean companion interpreted, and Manuel's smile faded as he regarded the massive, dark man at the fire-ring.

His companion was nervous and spoke swiftly in Spanish. Manuel continued to stand staring toward the dark man, holding his knife. The dark man started forward slowly and purposefully. The lean man grabbed Manuel's knife-arm and pulled his friend away. That ended it. Manuel put up his knife, lost interest in Tom Lee, and as he walked toward the base of the bluff with his companion he looked back twice where the dark man was filling a tin cup with coffee at the fire-ring.

By the time Lew rolled over and sat up, with a dull throbbing sensation in the back of his head, the Mexicans had carried twelve long crates over near the area in front of the wagon's tailgate, and stacked them.

Sam, Slim and the dark man remained over near the fire-ring and made no move to help. Bill Smith and the lean Mexican stood side by side at the tailgate, silent as they watched the working detail bring more crates over and stack them.

Reg was stirring when the lean Mexican said, '*martillo*' and someone handed him a claw-hammer which he used to prise the lids of three crates and stand gazing at their contents.

Bill Smith dryly said, 'The same. Still packed in grease. Altogether, two hunnert spankin' new Winchesters worth every bit what you pay for them.' Smith leaned to lightly kick the bottom crate, which was larger than the others, and which had been banded with steel. 'That's your widow-maker, Colonel. Shoots two hunnert an' fifty bullets a minute. What does that amount to in a Messican army; one company of riflemen? Two hunnert slugs a minute with just one man turning the crank.'

The lean Mexican stepped back to eye the lower crate. Lew was rubbing the back of his neck to stimulate circulation in the area where he had been struck. He could forget his headache. He did not even notice Reg get up into a sitting position as he gingerly felt the side of his face where he had been slugged by the powerfully-built dark man. Lew knew what a Gatling gun was because he had seen two or three of them, but had never seen one in use, although he understood exactly what they could do.

More than that, as he listened and looked, the astonishment which had held him rooted when he had lifted the lid off that big box in the

68

wagon, held him motionless now. Smith did not simply buy the loot from Mexican churches, he either traded for it, giving weapons in exchange, or he sold the looted treasure, bought weapons for the Mexicans, and kept the difference between what he sold the priceless antiques for, and what he paid for the weapons.

Reg muttered, attracting Lew's attention. He turned and saw the discoloration and swelling. He had not been conscious when his partner had also been knocked senseless. Lew jutted his jaw in the direction of the wagon. Reg left off feeling his painful injury and glanced over where the Mexicans were stacking the last crates.

With the work done the Mexicans returned to the centre of the camp, sweaty, hungry, and thirsty. Sam and Slim joined the muscular dark man at the fire-ring. They conversed in lowered voices while Bill Smith and the lean Mexican remained over at the tailgate.

Tom brought a canteen over and knelt between his friends as they drank. When Reg passed the canteen back, Lee said, 'I guess now it ain't hard to understand what that feller meant when he said wouldn't none of us be alive tomorrow.'

Sam strolled over and stood gazing at Lew, his eyes showing hatred. Without warning he hauled back one foot and aimed a kick. Lew had enough time to understand what was happening. He twisted away and reached with both hands, caught the ankle as it came within inches, and threw himself backward. Sam squawked and went down on his back with Lew coming up now, still holding the ankle. He swung the leg violently, and Sam's body was twisted half-over. With enough time to regain his feet, Lew sprang up, stepped ahead, and as Sam was frantically struggling to right himself, Lew dropped upon Sam's back with both knees. Sam's breath rattled out, his body arched, fell back, and both sets of fingers scrabbled at the ground as Sam's eyes bulged while he struggled hard to get his breath back.

The thick, dark man started toward Lew. His head seemed to grow directly out of his shoulders. If there was a neck it was a very short one.

Reg twisted to get upright, as did Tom Lee, but Reg's injured foot hampered him as he tried to move directly into the path of the oncoming Smith-rider. The *arrieros* began to hoot and shout encouragement. This was the sort of thing they thrived on.

Tom Lee ignored the oncoming juggernaut of a man. He stepped over where Sam was desperately trying to catch his breath, caught Sam from behind by his shellbelt and trouser-belt, lifted him off the ground and flung him like a log against the legs of the oncoming dark man.

The dark man sprawled face forward. Sam,

70

finally getting some air into his lungs, grabbed for something, anything at all, got a two-handed hold on the dark man's clothing, and clung like a leech with the dark man furiously trying to break away.

Bill Smith stormed through the Mexicans, about half of whom were doubled over with laughter while the other half hooted disdainfully at the dark man and Sam. Smith stopped, glaring at his prisoners, then he turned and snarled in a whiplash tone at his riders, who were finally getting disengaged so that they could arise.

One particular *arriero* hooted at the dark man. He was the ape-like small man with the knife who had been growled at earlier. He had not forgotten that, and now that the dark man had been made to look ridiculous, the Mexican was enjoying every moment of it.

Bill Smith was angry. For once, when he spoke, there were no intervals of long silence. He would stand for no fighting at the camp, he said, and until everything else had been taken care of, Sam and the dark man, whom Smith called Joe, were to stay away from the captives. They would, he told Sam and the dark man, be taken care of after sunrise, when the pack train was on its way.

An hour later two Mexicans brought some tortillas and carne con chili over where Lew, Reg and Tom were sitting on the ground. One

71

of the Mexicans was the ape-like man who had offered to fight Tom earlier. Now, he grinned widely at Tom, and reached over to feel one of Tom Lee's biceps. He and his lean partner were delighted over what had happened.

Other Mexicans walked past and also smiled. After they had eaten Lew said, 'Tom, couple more stunts like that and they'll make you *presidente* of all Arizona.'

Lee ignored that. 'You know what they got over there?'

Lew knew, so did Reg.

Tom looked at the distant crates. 'If one of us had walked past the wagon to the cliff, we'd have seen them gun boxes.'

Neither Lee nor Reg disputed that. They were each rolling a smoke.

'Smith had them crates cached,' Tom said, still having trouble putting it all together in his mind.

'He don't just buy that stolen Mex church stuff ... This here is the first bunch of gun-smugglers I ever saw.'

Lew turned the conversation to what the Mexican officer had told Bill Smith when he had handed over the payroll pouch. He then said, 'Twenty Mexicans on horseback leading twenty pack mules leave a trail a hundred yards wide that a blind man could follow.'

Tom looked blank.

'They killed a driver and a gunguard to rob

that stagecoach, and even if they did it a hundred miles from here, somewhere down their back-trail they stirred up a nest of hornets.'

Tom still looked blank.

'There is a posse tracking them,' Lew explained, and watched the expression of dawning understanding spread across Tom's face.

Reg blew smoke and said, 'That's not going to do us a damned bit of good.'

Bill Smith strolled up and stood gazing at the seated men, jaws slowly moving on his tobacco cud. 'If you figured to be clever,' he said in that calm drawling tone of voice, 'you should have left the country.'

Reg cocked an unfriendly eye upwards. 'You're right. Seems to me your Messican friends got as much of a problem as we have.'

Smith chewed, eyed Reg, and eventually said, 'How?'

'They go back toward the border the way they came up here, and they're going to run into a buzz-saw. Killing two men to rob a stagecoach will have every lawman between them and the border pounding leather with a posse.'

Bill Smith chewed, and thought, and finally turned on his heel to go back over where his riders and the Mexicans were eating, drinking, and making desultory conversation in two languages. Lew and Reg watched him take the

Mexican colonel to one side.

Reg smiled, and winced because that made his jaw hurt. 'It's not much of a consolation,' he told his companions, 'but it's about the best we're likely to get.'

Lew, who had been watching the crowd of men over in the vicinity of the cooking fire, saw several men toss meat scraps to the dog, and occasionally, when a man would leave the camp to disappear beyond lantern-light, the dog would sneak in and grab food off a tin plate. The Mexicans who noticed this laughed about it, but at least twice when the men who had left returned and found their food gone, they swore angrily and the dog would slink back toward the wagon. He was over there when Smith and the Mexican officer started back toward the fire.

Lew lost interest in the dog and as Smith and the Mexican came closer, with light on their faces, Lew recognised the looks of resentment on the faces of both men. Evidently Smith had not only relayed what Reg had said, but had also let the Mexican know what he thought of those two murders and the robbery.

CHAPTER EIGHT

THE BARKING DOG

The Mexican *arrieros*—packers—were not going to load up until morning, so they went about pitching their bedding in places which seemed suitable, and, like all Mexicans, they called back and forth in Spanish, sometimes making jokes, sometimes calling amusing insults, sometimes bursting out with short verses or ribald songs in Spanish.

Bill Smith and his three companions remained at the fire-ring with the Mexican officer, sipping bitter coffee and talking. When the Mexican finally tossed the dregs from his cup into the dying fire and arose to go hunt up his bedroll, Bill Smith methodically cut off a corner of his plug, placed it carefully into his mouth, looked around where the lumpy shapes were scattered, and quietly spoke to Joe, Slim and Sam.

'He wants another load next month. The revolution was starting before he left last month. They're going to need mostly ammunition next time . . . We got to find another meeting place.'

The muscular dark man called Joe was lounging on the ground when Smith said that, and asked a desultory question. 'Why? What difference does it make if those damned horse trappers found us? We'll bury them come morning.'

Smith was irritable this evening. 'It's not them, damn it. Some of his men saw a stagecoach and attacked it for a lark. They killed the driver and guard, dumped the coach into an arroyo, and brought back the bullion pouch. That's it lyin' yonder.'

The dark man was still unimpressed. 'Where?'

Smith spat into the coals. 'The colonel said at least a hunnert miles from here. But the point is, Joe, they killed those men last week, and there will be posses out hunting for the killers . . . A man could follow their tracks on a dark night. That many riders leading mules would leave tracks over rock. As soon as we get 'em loaded and gone, we bury the mustangers, then hitch up the wagon and head west, and the next camp's got to be a long way from here.'

Sam was sitting cross-legged with his head down, scowling. Now he raised it. 'Hell, if they track the Messicans to this camp, what's to stop them from trackin' us an' the wagon, no matter where we go?'

Bill Smith said, 'Blankets,' and tossed aside his tin cup without explaining. He arose, considered the prisoners, then tiredly said, 'Joe, tie those bastards. Tie 'em like turkeys. See you in the morning.'

76

Sam and Slim would have accompanied the muscular, dark man but when he arose to do as he had been told, he shook his head and said, 'Turn in. I don't need any help.'

Slim was willing but Sam wasn't. 'I'll lend a hand anyway,' he said, looking malevolently beyond the fire.

Joe was adamant. 'No sir. You're not goin' to start another fight.'

'I'm going to kill that son of a bitch that hit me, Joe.'

The dark man did not relent. 'All right. But not tonight. You can do whatever you want to do in the morning.'

Joe walked over to the prisoners with a coil of rope in his left hand, his sixgun in his right hand. He was impersonal and businesslike. 'Lie flat and roll over onto your bellies,' he commanded. Lew and Tom obeyed. So did Reg, but he was a little slower.

The burly man made his bindings tight, his knots doubled. He was evidently no novice at something like this. Afterwards, he rolled each man over onto his back and knelt looking at them. He looked longest at Reg. He did not smile, nor sneer, nor show any particular hostility. He was evidently a capable, deadly individual who did things like this in a detached frame of mind. He said, 'You boys got all night to pray.'

Lew had a question. 'How good is the pay?'

The dark man eyed Lew calmly. 'Pretty fair. A lot better'n running wild horses or fooling with cattle.'

'You need any more men?'

Finally, the dark man's stolid features changed expression. He smiled. 'I don't blame you for trying,' he said, and stood up to walk away.

The camp got quiet, smoke-scent lingered from the dying fire, Lew tried to sit up and failed, then rolled up onto one side so he would see his companions, and had to hitch one shoulder to push a piece of cooked meat aside where it had fallen when they had been fed.

Tom Lee spoke quietly. 'Strange how things happen, ain't it? My grandfather was shot to death by a firing squad a few hunnert miles from here. Up at Mountain Meadows. You fellers ever hear about the massacre of emigrants up there by the Mormons?'

Neither Reg nor Lew had heard about a massacre, and at this particular time they were not very interested, so neither of them answered.

That encouraged Tom to also say, 'His name was John Doyle Lee. He had a whole corralful of wives. Something like fifteen of 'em ... He was the man who organised that killing ... What strikes me as being strange is that he was shot to death up there, and here lies his grandson about to get the same treatment down

78

here.'

If either Reg or Lew saw anything strange or ironic in this, they did not say so. Reg rolled sideways and whispered to Lew. 'I'll sidle over and turn so's you can get a hand into my britches pocket. I got a clasp knife in the left pocket.'

Tom paused in his reverie to listen to this, then jack-knifed around so he could watch with interest how this was going to work.

It did not work. Lew's hands could reach the pocket but could not enter it because both hands would have to reach into the pocket, and the pocket was not that large. But Lew strained and tried different ways to get at the clasp knife, and Reg got more exasperated as time passed. When Lew finally lay back breathing hard from his efforts, Reg said, 'Try working it up with both hands from the outside. Maybe it'll fall out.'

Lew crabbed around into position to make the effort, and after watching for a few minutes, Tom whispered, 'You'll never make it that way ... Lew, wiggle over here and shove up my pantsleg. I got a boot-knife.'

Both Bentley and Palmer stared a long time at the big Mormon before Reg finally hissed at him. 'Damn you, Tom. Why didn't you say that fifteen minutes ago!'

'Well, you fellers was trying to get the pocket-knife out, that's why.'

Getting the boot-knife out required only a few

moments. Not all range men carried them, and the farther one got from the Mex border, the rarer such men became. But in the South Desert country it was not unusual to find cowboys who had sheath-knife scabbards sewn into the outside of their riding boots' inner lining, where the scabbard would not be rubbed against their leg by the stirrup leather.

Tom's knife had an eight-inch blade with a Bowie hook at its upper tip. Lew inch-wormed back where he had crawled from holding the boot-knife tightly in one fist. Over there, with Reg and Tom watching, he squirmed around until he could see the distant stone-ring, the slumbering lumps scattered around between the ring and the wagon. If anyone was watching, Lew could not make them out, so he eased up to face away, and after dropping the knife three times, and with sweat drenching his shirt, he got Tom's knife reversed for sawing, and went to work. He frequently had to halt to rest and shake sweat out of his eyes. The knife was not sharp. At least it was not as sharp as Lew wished it might be, and it was extremely difficult and tiring work, trying to cut through bindings of hard-twist lass rope.

A Mexican arose, spat, then ambled away from the camp to pee. Until he returned the prisoners had to feign sleep, and wait. When he shuffled back, scratching, and sought out his blankets again, Reg whispered, 'Hurry up.'

Lew whispered back, 'Shut up and lie still!'

At best he could only saw up and down over the rope in three inch strokes, and it seemed to take forever before he felt a strand part and fall slackly aside. He tried to strain enough to work the other loops free, but evidently the loop he had finally cut through was beneath other loops, and they kept the severed loop from yielding, so he had to grit his teeth and start all over again.

Tom Lee did not move but Reg fidgeted twice before Lew felt the second loop part, and this time when he strained, the binding loosened enough for him to get both hands free.

He lay back with aching joints, sweating and exhausted. After a while he rolled soundlessly over and looked at Reg, who was staring back. Lew smiled, but his partner did not smile back.

Lew cut the ankle bindings without sitting up to do it in case someone over yonder might be awake, then he very carefully rolled over twice, until he was directly behind Bentley.

This time, the cutting went faster. When it was finished Lew pushed his head close and said, 'Don't move.'

He motioned for Tom to turn his back. While he was freeing the big Mormon, one of the *arrieros* coughed, sat up and coughed harder until a nearby friend said, in Spanish, 'Shut up your mouth, damn it!'

The cougher gasped his answer, 'There's something in my throat.'

81

'May you die with it in your throat so the rest of us can get some rest!'

The cougher pushed out of his blankets, went to the coffeepot, poured some black liquid in a cup and stood drinking slowly to dislodge whatever it was which had made him cough. Afterward, with the coffee cup empty, he continued to stand there waiting to see if the coughing would resume. It didn't. He stepped over two big snoring lumps of men who had not been disturbed by his racket and got back down into his blanket. The nearby man he had awakened was still indignant.

'It is always something with you, Dominguez!'

'Go to sleep.'

'How can I? You brought me wide awake.'

'Go to sleep anyway. I didn't do it on purpose. Don't you ever have to cough?'

The conversation ended with the cougher having the last word. Some yards distant, upon the opposite side of the camp, Lew resumed his cutting. When he had Tom's wrists free, he sat up to cut their ankle bindings, and the dog came ambling over, perhaps more perceptive than his owner, or the packers who were sleeping and snoring across the camp in the vicinity of the stacked Winchester crates.

Reg and Tom shed the last of their ropes. Lew tossed the boot-knife over in front of its owner, and Tom methodically raised his trouser-leg to sheath the thing.

The dog came up to Lew wagging its tail. He reached to pat it on the back, and remembered that scrap of meat he had encountered earlier. He found it, closed it inside his left hand and with the dog's nose wrinkling because it had detected the scent of meat, Lew looked around, then jerked his head to lead the crawling and silent exodus as the three men went due west, in the same direction from which they had originally approached the camp.

Lew's heart was pounding. At any moment now someone back there might sit up and notice that the prisoners were gone. If that happened, no matter how fast the escapees crawled, or even jumped up and ran, it was highly improbable that when the camp was roused and all those armed men ran forth seeking them, they could reach their tethered horses before they were riddled.

Finally, Lew tossed the meat scrap to the dog, who snatched it up and turned back in the direction of the wagon. Reg and Tom stood up and followed when Lew started running.

They had a lot of ground to cover. They had stalked about a mile and a half to approach the camp, and now they had that same distance to retreat over.

Tom's crooked foot slowed him, but he probably would not have been able to run any faster without it. He was large, heavy-boned and was neither built nor coordinated for covering ground fast while on foot.

Reg did better. Even so, with the swelling gone from his injured toe, it still pained him to put weight on it. But the pain was not a consideration to Bentley, who was a very pragmatic individual; the alternative to not running swiftly was a bullet in the back. He ran almost as swiftly as Lew did.

When they found the horses, which had been dozing despite the thirst which had begun to bother them about sundown, it only required moments to get the reins free, the saddles snugged up and, finally, for the escapees to spring across saddle leather.

At about the same time someone let out a great bawling shout back at the wagon-camp. The fact that the prisoners had escaped had been discovered.

This time it was Tom Lee on his big animal who took the lead and did not slacken his gait even when he had to ride through a boulder field.

The sounds back yonder diminished as the mustangers continued to head back in the direction of their box-canyon camp. When Tom finally reined up to listen for pursuit, Reg said, 'Go east or west, Tom. They're goin' to head for our camp sure as hell.'

Lew acted as though he had not been listening as he sat forward and raised a big arm to point with. 'They're coming,' he announced, and turned almost due west as he held the lead. But from here on, perhaps because the big Mormon did not feel the same need for haste, he rode at a kidney-jarring trot.

They covered about two miles before he halted a second time. They were silent while they waited to detect the sound of many angry horsemen passing up-country. But they were too distant to hear anything but the faint barking of an excited dog.

Tom grinned as he said, 'He's helping.'

The dog was doing exactly that. As he raced along beside his owner, barking excitedly, it was possible for the mustangers to track the progress of the pursuit by sound. Clearly, Bill Smith was leading his horsemen in the direction of the cul-de-sac canyon, exactly as Reg has predicted.

Tom was sitting his horse grinning widely as he listened, but neither of his companions grinned, spoke, nor took a very deep breath for a full ten minutes, until the barking dog's sound was very faint. Then Lew raised both arms above his head and worked his shoulders because they ached from being tied, and from his other efforts before they had got free.

CHAPTER NINE

BEREFT

They were without weapons, riding thirsty horses, and although they had canteens on their saddles, that was about all they had, and dawn was not far off when Lew called for a halt. He was of the opinion that they had travelled west far enough.

Tom thought so too, and he was grinning when he shocked his companions with his proposal about what they should do next.

'Go back down there. All them fellers is out lookin' for us. Well, maybe they left a man or two with the wagon, but I'll bet you fellers a new hat it ain't no more'n that, and most likely they didn't leave nobody.' He paused to watch their reactions. Reg gazed sulphurously at the big Mormon without opening his mouth. Lew started to say 'you're crazy' but closed his mouth just in time.

It was a good idea. Maybe a little crazy, certainly dangerous, but on the other hand there was water down there, and food, and no one but another crazy man was going to think they might go back down to the wagon-camp.

'Don't just set there,' growled Reg, flagging southward with an upflung arm.

Tom was still grinning when he turned down-country, and from this point on he only loped his horse where moonlight showed rock-free territory to lope over.

They got within a mile of the camp before Lew called a halt, flung his reins to Reg and trotted away on foot. He knew they had to be close, but he wanted to determine how close. He had no desire to ride up onto the camp in the poor light and get blown to Kingdom Come.

Although Tom Lee had angled slightly on their way back, he was still roughly a half-mile west of the big bluff, beyond which was the wagon-camp, and Lew had to trot that far, then back again, so that by the time he retrieved his reins and was ready to mount, he was fairly well tuckered out.

He pointed, and held a rigid finger to his lips. Tom nodded understanding of both gestures, and took the lead again. Back a few yards Reg was watching in all directions, but particularly in the direction of their back-trail. Without much doubt, if Smith and his riders came back southward after dawn on their way to the wagon-camp, they would notice three sets of shod-horse tracks going west, and he would bring all his companions over the back-trail.

Finally, they drew rein behind the same barranca which had the wagon-camp around front. They were several hundred yards away from the camp, left their horses hobbled because there was nothing to tie them to, and began the long stalk toward the front of the bluff.

They were fortunate as much because the moon was leaving as because the earth was soft and dusty from millennia of too little rainfall. It was easy getting around to the upper end of the bluff, then down along the base as far as the rope corral where pack mules already had their long ears pointing like aerials because they had detected man-scent and were now waiting for the movement which invariably followed such a scent.

But the mules were interested, not particularly worried; they'd had all this long night to grow accustomed to the smell of strange men coming and going, so when Reg limped over to look in at them, the mules simply looked back as motionless as rocks. They did not bray. In fact they scarcely moved at all as Tom and Lew came up.

Reg turned to whisper, 'Two horses.'

The implication was that there would be two men still at the camp. Lew motioned for his companions to remain where they were. He got over to the wagon and down the south side of it until he could sweep the entire area of the camp with its flung-aside blankets and scattered horse and mule gear until he saw, not two men, but just one man over at the fire-ring where he was concentrating on starting a little fire.

It had turned chilly.

Lew waited a long while, watching the man and looking for his companion, but since no other man appeared he went back to tell Reg and Tom what he had seen, then to lead them back.

The little fire was spluttering to life. Because it had been built of dry old dead limbs of underbrush it burned very hot, and by the time it got into full fury, it would also burn brightly but without smoke.

The lone man at the fire-ring had his back to the wagon. He had no idea he was not alone. Nor did he stop worrying over the little fire until the three men were less than fifteen feet behind him. Then he straightened back with both hands extended to the increasing heat, and Tom tapped Reg and Lew as he stepped silently past them, grinning.

The stalk was a complete success, up until Tom leaned from behind to grab a handful of shirt-cloth. At that precise moment the man leaned forward and rocked up to his feet, and turned. By firelight Reg and Lew saw the expression on his face when he turned and met Tom Lee's wide grin. The man's jaw sagged, his eyes bulged, his entire body went momentarily rigid with surprise. If it had been either Lew or Reg, they would have struck him senseless in that one moment when the man was too stunned to move. But it was Tom, and his reactions were slower.

The *arriero* had a squat, thick body, a neck which arose directly from sloping shoulders for no more than two or three inches, then was topped by an ape-like head with a sloping forehead and a thick, coarse jaw. But the Mexican's reflexes were perfect. He did not swing, he instead took one backward step with his right hand moving. Tom went after him swinging. He missed the first blow but the second one connected. The squatty Mexican grunted and almost went down. His right hand was rising as Lew sprang ahead, sixgun rising as he cocked it. The Mexican saw Lew, saw the gun even as his hand flipped back with a thick-bladed knife rising into poised position for the overhand throw. The man hesitated. The only time he did that. Tom hit him squarely on the point of the jaw. The knife went one way, the *arriero* went a different way.

Lew slowly holstered his Colt. When Reg walked up they exchanged a glance then Tom was bending to retrieve the big knife. He straightened around, smiling.

They went through the camp but did not find the other man, if there had ever been one. Tom went back to fetch in their saddle animals to be watered while Reg and Lew put their backs to the little fire enjoying its heat before they spread out and rummaged the camp.

They tied the unconscious Mexican to a

wagon wheel, disarmed him, and went back to help with their horses. Later, when they were eating food from the wagon, Reg said, 'We could build another fire beside those gun boxes and turn the animals loose.'

There were a number of things they could do. What troubled Lew was all that massively heavy gold and jewelled treasure in the wagon. They would have no difficulty taking the payroll pouch away with them, but the infinitely more valuable church treasure was many times heavier than the pouch. Even if they wasted a couple more hours rigging up the pack mules to carry the treasure, as heavy as it was, they would be unable to move fast with it, and shortly now dawn would come. After that, the men with Bill Smith would probably return. By daylight, they could easily follow the sign left by Tom, Reg and Lew, and in a horse race, the mustangers would lose as long as they were burdened. This kind of a race would result in the mustangers getting shot to death on sight.

Nor did they dare set fire to the carbine crates which were stacked close to the wagon's tailgate, because the wagon would certainly also burn, and that would result in all those priceless old church implements melting down.

Lew said, 'We'll take the money pouch and drive the mules along for a few miles, then leave them. And we'd better start moving soon.'

Neither Reg nor Tom argued. Tom had not

looked into the treasure chests, but if he had it probably would not have aroused his cupidity—if he had any—and as far as Reg was concerned, he wanted to get away from the wagon-camp the moment he detected a hint of false dawn along the eastern rim of the world.

They rode past the bound *arriero* without a word. He raised dark eyes with muddy whites and watched them go. For a short while after they had departed the only sound was of driven mules foraging ahead of their herders in a strange land which they alternately tried to hasten through, and also slackened pace until the drivers had to use rommals to keep them moving.

Reg had the payroll pouch tied to his rear skirt. As the dawn filled out grudgingly and the cold increased, Reg would have traded the pouch and its contents for the old sheep-pelt lined horsehide coat he had left back at the wild-horse camp.

They turned the mules northward when they were more than a mile west, and pushed them over into a lope, a gait they held until the sun was on its way, then they abandoned the pack animals and struck out directly northward for the horse camp.

They did not get up there, at the lower, blocked-off end of the cul-de-sac canyon, until the sun was well above the horizon. Lew scouted until he found fresh tracks, going and coming, and killed time climbing to the barranca to look southward. He did not see Bill Smith and his riders, but there was a definite spindrift of dust hanging in the motionless air a considerable distance southward.

He went back and brought his companions up to their camp. The place had been savagely plundered. Everything worth stealing, including Reg Bentley's sheep-pelt lined horsehide coat, had been taken.

If Smith and his riders had still been there, they would have been attacked regardless of odds, but they were long gone.

Without speaking, the three men gathered what was left and watered the horses again, then paused long enough for two of them to smoke a cigarette, while bitterly viewing the ruin and devastation left by Smith and his men. Reg said, 'We should have kept their damned mules and taken them up to Saint George to sell.' He gestured. 'The sons of bitches even took our cooking pot and what was left of our sack of beans.' He looked from one of his friends to the other one, dropped his smoke, stamped savagely on it, and spoke again. 'Let's go back down there. I want a piece of someone's hide for this. And I want my horsehide coat back too.'

Lew inhaled, exhaled, dropped his quirley and without bothering to argue, headed for his horse. 'Ninety damned miles,' he said, swinging back into the saddle. 'Let's get started.'

93

Tom obediently mounted and reined over near Lew, but Reg was standing stubbornly beside his horse, glaring southward. 'I want that damned coat back,' he exclaimed.

Lew was already moving northward when he growled at his partner, 'Get on that danged horse and quit complaining. We'd never be able to sneak up on them again, even in the dark. Come along!'

Reg followed doggedly silent. Now and then he would glance back, but neither of his partners did. They had a long ride ahead. They also had nothing to show for the length of time they had put in down here. In fact they now had less than they had brought with them, and that was little enough.

Except for the pouch.

By midday when they had covered a fair amount of ground, almost fifteen miles, they had heat to contend with, and no water.

But they rested in a shadowed deep arroyo with crumbly banks, and down there Lew methodically slit one side of the money pouch with Tom's boot-knife.

The amount of paper money was incredible. None of them had ever seen more than a hundred or two dollars at any one time in their lives. Lew fished forth one handful and counted six hundred dollars. It was crisp, new money, as though it had gone from the mint where it was manufactured, to whatever bank it had been earmarked for.

Tom gazed at it in disgust and said, 'They couldn't spend that stuff. It's too clean and unwrinkled and all. It looks counterfeit it's so perfect.'

Reg reached for a few notes and studied them intently before raising his eyes to Lew. 'Do you think it's counterfeit?'

Lew did not think so. 'If it was a payroll for some big company or mine, or maybe an army post, sure as hell it might be new, but it sure wouldn't be counterfeit.'

Reg considered the notes again for a moment then handed them back with a grunt and a growl. 'Counterfeit or not I think we're entitled at least to enough of it to replace what we lost or got stolen. How much would you guess might be in there, Lew?'

Palmer had anticipated that question from one of them. 'I'd guess maybe five, six thousand dollars. Maybe seven or eight thousand.'

No one made a sound for a long time, not until Lew decided it was time to push on again, then Reg stood up beating off dust as he said, 'For that kind of money no one would ever miss say two or three hunnert.'

Lew was in the saddle turning up out of the arroyo with the pouch tied behind his cantle when he replied to his partner. 'My guess is that whoever lost this money, knows right down to the last *centavo* how much is in the pouch.'

95

'Well,' exclaimed Reg, unwilling to yield. 'How about a reward for us for recovering it?'

'It'll be up to whoever lost it . . . Do either of you fellers remember any water up through here?'

Tom answered. He knew this country. 'Not until maybe tomorrow afternoon. There's an old Mormon well at a deserted old tumble-down tiny settlement called Wolf Hole.'

Reg looked darkly around. 'By tomorrow afternoon we'll likely be riding dead horses,' he said, and Tom laughed, then turned merry blue eyes upon Bentley.

'That's plumb silly, Reg. You can't ride a dead horse.'

Reg, and Lew as well, turned to gaze at the big Mormon, baffled by the fact that Tom had been able to contribute so much to their miraculous escape, and now rode along looking at them as though *they* were a few bricks shy of a load.

CHAPTER TEN

WIND

By dusk, with the heat beginning to diminish, they had covered a fair distance without pushing their animals, which they could not do, and when they made a dry camp out in open country where there were no arroyos in sight, Tom Lee scarfed around and came up with an armload of twigs for a fire because a little ground-wind was beginning to blow.

The horses could have used a drink but they were not suffering. Yet, anyway, but by tomorrow afternoon they would be and that worried all three mustangers. Tom explained about the little two or three building settlement to the west called Wolf Hole. He also cautioned against rising hopes by mentioning that he had not been over there in a number of years, and for all he knew now, the place could have burned down or been abandoned.

Reg was not moved by whatever kind of disaster might have overtaken Wolf Hole. 'The well had ought to still be there.'

Tom agreed, and as the little wind increased, became steady and annoying, Reg also moaned about the loss of his horsehide coat, and one of their hobbled animals picking underbrush-shoots to the east, threw up its head and nickered.

There was no time to kick dirt over the fire. They sprang up and sprinted beyond the reach of its light, and stood out there listening for the sound of whatever had aroused the animal's interest, each of them wondering whether it was Bill Smith again, perhaps determined to track them down, this time, for the money pouch they had taken.

Lew said, 'I've never felt so damned helpless in my life.' He meant without guns. Reg was cold and getting colder because the wind was beginning to go through him, and it too was getting colder. Of all the things rangemen had no love for, wind topped the list. Heat, cold, even drought, could be borne, but wind not only immobilised them, made it impossible to work and accomplish much, it also wore a man out bracing each time it hit him.

The little fire burned brightly, agitated by the wind. It appeared as a tiny beacon, the only vestige of light visible in the darkness.

The moon had not arrived by the time Tom wearied of standing out there and suggested they go back to the warmth. Lew was reluctant to do that. 'If someone's around, sure as hell they'll be lying out a-ways waiting for us to do just exactly that . . . If it's Smith we'll get shot like birds on a fence.'

Tom said no more, but he swung his arms and stamped his feet. Reg saw no future in just standing out in the darkness. 'Anything is better'n doing nothing. Suppose we fan out and do a little scouting . . . For Christ's sake be careful.'

Lew went northward. Reg and Tom turned southward where they intended to split up, each going in a different direction, and as long as the moon did not arrive, they had plenty of darkness to conceal their movement. Also, although the ground was soft which meant they probably would not make much noise as they moved, what really helped was the wind. It carried sound away.

Lew wanted to get over near the hobbled horses. He thought that if anyone was indeed trying to ambush their camp, he would try to stay between the horses and the little fire in order to be in a good position if the mustangers tried to get to their animals for escape.

It was good logic, but when he got over where he could kneel and skyline their horses, the animals were browsing as though nothing had troubled them.

Lew considered the possibility of coyotes or foxes, or perhaps an itinerant big cat passing through. But none of those things would have made that horse whinny the way he had. Then the idea hit Lew: The horse would have made that particular kind of whinny if it had been wild-horse scent he had picked up. If it was wild horses out there somewhere in the darkness, there was nothing to fear.

He sat on the ground watching those dim silhouettes as their mounts moved near some underbrush. The question was: Could Smith, or whatever his name was, and his riders, have got up this far between the time they returned and found the pouch gone, and the time Reg, Lew and Tom had struck their base camp and ridden this far northward?

For Smith it was a hell of a distance, and horses were not machines. The longer he crouched out there, the more he began to doubt that it was Smith and his renegades.

An owl-hoot was borne softly upon the wind. Lew did not move except to turn his head in the direction of that sound. A man who had spent most of his life in range country knew that while owls called back and forth in forested country at night, in the desert where they did not live in trees, but in ground burrows, they did not hoot at night. They hunted, skimming silently a few feet above the ground searching for night-feeding rodents, and no owl, not even the high-country variety, hooted while in flight.

Indians used bird sounds to signal one another, and Tom had said something about there being a few Indians down here, but Lew discarded that idea almost as soon as it occurred to him. Not entirely because he also knew Indians did not raid much at night, because he also knew that some tribes of Southwestern Indians in fact did raid at night. He discarded the idea because he intuitively felt it was not redskins, it was whiteskins out there somewhere; men who had perhaps seen their fire, had been attracted to it in the darkness, and had ridden as close as they dared before piling off to finish their stalk on foot.

The hair at the back of his neck stood straight

100

up. If it wasn't redskins, and it wasn't Smith, then who the hell was it? Unless they did not intend to be friendly they would not be acting the way they were, either.

Lew wished for the dozenth time he had a weapon.

The horses stopped browsing to stand motionless as they peered northward. Lew watched, and hoped very hard neither Reg nor Tom would suddenly walk up where Lew was sitting.

They didn't, and the horses did not go back to browsing either. Whoever was out there was approaching, probably to remove the hobbles and run off the horses, which was the time-honoured method of putting enemies at a man's mercy in this kind of country.

Lew made his decision. Whatever else happened, he could not allow someone to put them afoot. He moved forward a yard at a time, sank to the ground at intervals to look and listen, then slipped ahead again.

There were fist-sized rocks all around. He had to be careful of them. There was also scraggly underbrush, not very tall and blessed—or cursed—with inch-long thorns. He utilised the brush to mask his movement until he was within a stone's throw of their saddle animals. Once, Tom Lee's big roan glanced in Lew's direction, but only for a moment, then he faced northward again.

Lew said nothing. No movement, no man-shapes. Nor did the owl hoot again. Behind him some distance, the little fire had been wind-whipped until it had almost burned down to coals. There was no sign of either Reg or Tom, but once he heard two rocks roll together on his right, and slightly to the rear, down where he thought one or the other of his partners would be. But when he looked, and waited, nothing appeared.

He had never favoured boot-knives, but as he crouched out there in the cold wind, he would have felt much better if he'd been carrying one.

Tom's big roan sucked back a little and softly snorted. Lew flattened against the ground like a lizard when a silhouette seemed to rise up out of the earth between him and the roan gelding. It was a man wearing a dark coat, with an old hat tugged so low it reached his ears. He was wearing shiny old shotgun chaps and leather gloves, and he was concentrating his full attention upon the horses.

The distance was perhaps sixty-five feet. The man crouched forward, waiting for the roan horse to loosen up a little. All three horses were hobbled, which implied that they could be approached, and caught, with ease, but the fact of the matter was different; any horse who had been wearing hobbles for a long period of time, learned to hop with them on his ankles much faster than a two-legged creature could run to

102

catch up. Evidently the man in the crushed hat knew this. In fact his appearance reinforced Lew's observation that the stranger was a seasoned and experienced range man.

Lew arose from the ground without a sound, being very careful as he got up into a crouch and moved toward the man whose back was to him. He was relying entirely upon the roan horse, and the animal gave assistance without knowing he was doing it. He shuffled backward a couple of feet, then stood braced with most of his weight off his front end so that he could whirl in a second. Lee closed almost half the distance when the man began to talk soothingly to the roan horse in little more than a whisper.

Lew covered the final distance, picked up a round fist-sized rock, took two more wide steps, and hurled the stone. It did not strike the man's head as Lew had intended, but it hit him in the back of the neck with similar results: the man dropped to his knees, evidently stunned rather than knocked senseless. Lew reached, grabbed coarse cloth and wrenched the man half around with his left hand, while firing his right fist. This time the man collapsed in a heap, and the roan horse whirled and hopped frantically eastward, frightening the other two horses, which followed him through the darkness.

Lew wasted no time with the unconscious man. He yanked him over, grabbed the sixgun from the man's holster, shoved it into his waistband, then roughly yanked off the man's old coat.

Armed again, and protected from the cold wind, he used both belts, the one holding the empty holster, and the one which normally supported the stranger's britches, to bind his prisoner's arms behind his back and to truss his ankles as well.

Then he turned swiftly southward to locate his partners, leaving the unconscious stranger where he had fallen.

Undoubtedly there was more than one man out there in the darkness. Perhaps the unconscious man's friends would find him. Lew needed to locate Tom and Reg first.

The way he found Lee was the same way he had found that stranger. Without warning as Lew was hastening soundlessly southward, something big and thick launched itself at him from the darkness, hit him with the force of a locomotive and knocked him sprawling. He was briefly stunned, but instinct told him to fight back, and he did, but Tom had the advantage. He straddled Lew with a big fist pulled back. He did not fire it. Instead he leaned down, staring, then he said, 'Where did you find the coat?' and got off Palmer hauling him up to his feet as he arose.

Lew spat dirt and made certain the sixgun had not been dislodged, then he explained what he had encountered northward and easterly where the horses had been, and they both went back to the area where Tom had last seen Reg.

Reg was belly-down sky-lining. He recognised big Tom Lee, but not Lew until they were much closer, then he got to his feet eyeing the coat. 'Any more where that one came from?' he asked.

They spoke shortly, then turned back, but more eastward this time, over in the direction Lew had last seen their horses. Even if they had to abandon their saddles and what little remained of their personal gatherings, and had to flee bareback, the alternative seemed likely to be worse, and perhaps very final.

Cold made Lew shove both hands into coat pockets. He was walking when he did this, and abruptly halted dead in his tracks, looked down as he slowly pulled one hand out of a coat pocket, with his puzzled companions crowding close to see what had caused his halt.

There was a small nickel badge on his palm with a steel circlet around a five-pointed star. The legend on the steel circlet said 'United States Deputy Marshal'.

There was something engraved on the star too, but they could not make it out in the darkness. Reg's head came up slowly. He turned to gaze back in the direction from which they had just come. Tom took the badge and held it closer to his face, lips moving as he spelled out each word. Tom Lee had never read a book or a newspaper in his life, but he was not entirely incapable of reading. It just came hard to him.

When he handed back the badge he said, 'You expect it belongs to that feller you left tied up back yonder?'

Lew did not doubt that. What was bothering him was also bothering his partner. If there was a lawman-posse back there, why were they down here so far from anywhere? Reg said, 'Damn! They'll get to the camp and find that money pouch.' He faced his friends. 'We better find the horses and get to riding. I got a bad feeling if we call out an' try to explain, they're going to start shooting.'

Under the circumstances it was logical. They started walking again, more briskly now, in the direction their horses had taken.

It was a long walk, and once, faintly heard through the steady wind, they heard a man call, and another man answer him. Lew was certain the first call had come from their abandoned camp.

Tom saw his big roan. The other two horses were not far. Nor did the animals flee this time; they knew their owners. But having squaw-bridles fashioned out of trouser-belts and having men spring onto them bareback was a new experience. Few horses enjoyed being ridden bareback and no horse welcomed something put in his mouth which had been cured with oakbark acid. But these mounts were permitted no opportunity to express disapproval. Once the men were astride, they struck out northward and did not allow their animals to think unpleasant or rebellious thoughts. They loped for a solid hour, then as Tom began angling westerly toward that tiny settlement he had mentioned where they would find water, they slackened off to ride at a steady walk. By then the horses had decided to at least accept their unique predicament, and being ridden bareback did not bother them as much as it bothered the riders, especially when the horses trotted.

The moon arrived and miraculously, as though there were a connection, the wind stopped.

CHAPTER ELEVEN

'DON'T MOVE!'

Darkness remained but with moonlight it was a lot less dense. The three men riding bareback could see quite clearly for about a hundred yards, but there was nothing worthwhile to look at. Just rocks, an occasional plinth of wind-carved sandstone, one of those reddish-copper looking bluffs, boulders and underbrush. The rocks which were lying loose over here were smaller and much farther apart than they had been, back in the vicinity of the cul-de-sac canyon.

There did not appear to be any pursuit. At least each time they halted to look back and listen, there was no sign of pursuit.

The night did not warm up, but neither did it get any colder. A couple of times when they had to ride down into broad arroyos to reach the far side and continue in a direct line toward their destination, it was warm below ground level.

They had been riding three hours when they got a scare, when running horses beyond sight and slightly behind them made a noise like a troop of cavalry. But the fear passed as the horses made an obvious effort to get as far as they could from the man-scent.

Tom said, 'Mustangs.'

The moon sank and finally the chill increased. Reg swore and swung his arms. Lew, who was insulated against the cold, wondered how the man he had taken the coat from was making out. Probably not too well, and probably fit to be tied.

Just before dawn Tom straightened up gazing southward. Neither Reg nor Lew had heard or seen anything, but the big Mormon did not settle forward for a long time, and then he said, 'That's not wild horses this time.'

His companions still heard nothing, but an hour later with false dawn bringing enough light to make up for the departed full moon, they saw riders paralleling them southward. This time, Lew was willing to believe it was Smith and his renegades, and turned northward to get beyond view, in case they had not already been seen.

Evidently they hadn't because the distant shadows continued ahead without even a pause.

Lew halted, looked around, and said, 'Now what?'

Tom was not very worried. 'Unless they come north quite a ways they're goin' right past Wolf Hole, and if the sun don't rise right soon, they won't even see the place.'

It wasn't much, but they still had to find water, so Tom took the lead and continued the way they had been riding.

Reg rode beside his partner. 'If that was Smith, why would he be 'way over here? He'd make for the camp near the blind-canyon, or maybe he'd go due north because that'd be the sensible way for us to go—but what would make him even think we might be going west?'

Lee shrugged. He had no answer.

They found the village even though it was still not very light out. And it was not a village, just one long building which was a store, and a few outbuildings. Lew asked Tom why anyone would have a store where no one lived, and got a smile and a shrug for his answer. Tom did not know why the store was down here and clearly did not want to strain his mind trying to imagine a reason, but actually, the Wolf Hole store supplied the entire countryside as far east as the Short Creek settlement, and as far west as anyone cared to go. Northward, the next nearest store would be up at Saint George. Southward, there would be no store at all for hundreds of miles.

Lew looked for those riders who had passed them in darkness. There was no sign of them. In fact there was no visible sign of life at all, not even up ahead where that old weathered building stood. He stopped and sat his saddle. When Reg got impatient, Lew said, 'Look yonder, beyond that building. Open country. You see any riders out there? Neither do I and we can see a hell of a distance, maybe fifty miles.' Lew spat and straightened up. 'They either found a big hole in the ground and rode into it, Reg, or they're over by that long old building. Maybe behind it.'

Reg had been frustrated too many times lately to enjoy the prospect of being frustrated again. 'We got to have water for the horses,' he exclaimed. 'You want to sit out here all day? Those riders probably turned north.'

Tom soothed the situation by volunteering to ride over there, where he said the old woman who owned the place—if she still did—knew him. He would look around and come back. Meanwhile, Reg and Lew could go back as far as a sandstone spire, and wait out of sight until he

110

came back.

It was not a perfect idea, but then nothing had been perfect since the three of them had left Saint George to come down here. Tom was already riding away when Reg swung off and stood beside his horse as he said, 'You ever get the feeling that you're the only tree stump in the countryside, and everyone else is dogs?'

Lew piled off smiling. 'It could be worse,' he murmured, and Reg picked that up instantly.

'How? Just tell me how.'

Lew did not reply. Tom was small in the distance as he walked the big roan up to the rack out front of the long building. They saw him swing off, loop the reins and walk to the doorway. He disappeared inside.

Reg's stomach was grumbling. Everything they had brought south with them to eat was back in their abandoned camp. He rolled and lit a smoke, which was a poor substitute for breakfast, but the alternative was to hunker there with his back to the sandstone spire sucking air, which would be even less satisfying. He continued to squint far ahead where the roan horse stood hip-shot at the rack, and said, 'Maybe you were right.'

Lew turned his head. 'About what?'

'Being a stone mason ... I got this picture in my mind of you and me fifty years from now riding the same saddles and wearing pretty much the same clothes, still trying to get rich off wild horses. I don't think we got much of a future down here, Lew.'

A deep, rough voice spoke from behind them. 'I don't believe you got a future down here either. *Don't move!* Don't even turn your heads!'

He was not alone but neither Lew nor Reg saw the others until the man who had spoken in the rough deep voice sidled around to face them. He was holding a long-barrelled Colt which still had most of its original bluing. The hammer was all the way back. The man was as gaunt as a twig which made him look taller than he was. His eyes were sunk-set and his nose was beaked with flaring nostrils. He was the colour of old bronze, except for a pair of very blue eyes. He had grey over his ears and lines in his weathered face. He gestured with the cocked Colt. 'Throw that gun away, mister.'

Lew reach gingerly to lift out the gun in his waistband and toss it aside.

The thin man seemed to relax slightly. He said, 'Stand up.'

They both arose. Reg look sour and unafraid. 'Who the hell are you?' he growled.

The gaunt man did not reply. Two other men came around into view. The three of them must have been behind the plinth when Reg and Lew came back this far to wait. Evidently the waiting was now over. Over in front of the long building Tom emerged into sunlight and went as far as his tethered horse before stopping. There were

112

three men behind him, and although it was impossible at that distance to see what they had in their hands, a man did not hold his hand in quite that position unless he was aiming a gun.

One of the unshaven, stained and rumpled men looked back and grunted. 'They got him,' this man said to the gaunt individual. 'Now we got 'em all.'

The gaunt man looked squarely at Lew. 'Shed that coat, mister.' Lew obeyed and the gaunt man stepped ahead, picked up the coat and stepped back as he shrugged into it. His blue gaze was like ice. 'I owe you a couple,' he said to Lew, eased off the hammer and leathered the sixgun Lew had flung aside. He walked back and handed the weapon to the gaunt man, then held out his hand until the gaunt man handed over the sixgun he had dropped into his holster. This seemed to satisfy the man who had retrieved the sixgun. He walked past putting the gun into his empty holster while the gaunt man stood gazing at Reg and Lew.

Eventually he said, 'You boys overlooked something. They got a telegraph up at Saint George. And they got one down near Seward . . . Where are the Messicans?'

Lew was beginning to have a hunch. He made no attempt to answer the questions. He instead asked a question of his own. 'Who are you fellers?'

The gaunt man felt inside his coat pocket,

then said, 'You know who we are. You saw the badge ... Where are the Messicans who ride with you?'

'You caught the wrong men,' Lew stated. 'You found the money pouch at our camp. Right?'

'You're going to try and tell us some big tale,' stated the gaunt man.

'I'm going to tell you the truth,' stated Lew, and launched into a recitation of all that had occurred since the mustangs had been freed from their trap in the box canyon. By the time he had finished Tom Lee astride his big roan was almost back to where his companions were. Three silent, weathered men with harsh casts to their faces rode in Tom's wake.

Lew finished speaking, looked from face to face and saw no change in any of the expressions, and let go a long sigh of resignation.

Tom came up, swung off and looked sheepishly at his friends. 'You was right,' he exclaimed. 'These three was waiting for me inside the store, with their horses out back.'

A bandy-legged man approached the thin man. 'We better tank up back at the store, Marshal, before we head north. She's got a fair assortment of vittals too. Even tinned peaches.'

The marshal continued to study Reg and Lew as though his rider had not spoken. Eventually he said, 'Bill Smith ... ?'

Lew shrugged. 'He didn't tell us his name. We just hung that one on him.'

'How many Mex packers?'

'Fifteen that I counted. Maybe a couple more. And a big string of mules.'

'That one you said Smith called "colonel", what was his name?'

'I don't know. When they were around us they didn't call each other by name that I remember.'

'Describe Bill Smith.'

Lew obeyed with Tom nodding his head in agreement all the while. Then Tom added something else. 'The fellers with him are called Slim, Joe and Sam. Sam owns a dog. It was there with them.'

One of the listening men put a sardonic look upon the federal officer. 'I told you if these men were the men, they were shy one, Will.'

The marshal sent a man around the plinth for the horses, then relaxed a little as he stood in deep thought, ignoring the men around him. Finally he said, 'We're going south and look for sign. For your sake I hope you haven't been lying.'

Reg demurred. 'Not until we water our horses, mister, we're not going anywhere.'

That kind of defiance from unarmed men facing twice their number of men who were armed, made a grizzled, greying, squatty man laugh. Good-naturedly he took the reins of a horse from someone as he said, 'Marshal Tetford, you better let them water their horses,' then the grizzled man laughed again, and several of the other men grinned in appreciation of the rough joke.

The federal officer snapped an order. 'Get mounted.' When everyone was in the saddle he turned without another word and led the way over to the Wolf Hole store. Reg and Lew exchanged a glance; if Marshal Tetford had ever smiled it must have been long ago, perhaps when he had been a small child.

That same grizzled older man said, 'You boys like riding bareback?'

Reg threw back an answer. 'No, and we don't like being stalked by amateurs either.'

The grizzled man's patronising good nature dwindled. He reined away to ride with someone else.

Marshal Tetford led all the way. When they reached the store, a greying, dumpy woman was standing in the doorway of the store building. Behind her was a sturdily-built redheaded girl who was perhaps sixteen or eighteen years of age. The girl was interested in each rider, in turn, but her mother was interested in none of them.

CHAPTER TWELVE

HEAT, DUST, AND FEAR

Marshal Will Tetford was one of those people whose line of work ordinarily did not endear them to very many people, and as a result of that, he had developed a tough, resolute, cryptic manner. All the dumpy woman knew was that three men with badges had trapped a big, younger man in her store and had ridden away with him, and now those three, plus two bedraggled individuals riding bareback, and another trio of lawmen were back.

While the horses were being watered she waited on Marshal Tetford in her store, and once she made a tactless remark. She said, 'Folks down here don't cotton to outsiders,' and Tetford fixed her with his steady blue eyes when he replied. 'I don't know any folks down here, ma'am, and if you was to represent 'em, I don't think I'd want to ... Total up that bill and we'll be on our way.'

What he had bought were items rangemen rarely saw; tinned peaches, slabs of milk chocolate, and six cans of tinned milk the consistency of glue, which he handed around when they were riding away from Wolf Hole settlement. Neither Tetford nor the bandy-legged older deputy touched the milk. Tom and Reg got their share, and another posseman, tall, slightly hump-shouldered with a bulge of chewing tobacco in one cheek, handed his tin of milk to Lew, with a cryptic remark. 'I been weaned for forty-one years now.'

Reg wanted to return to the horse camp for their saddles and bridles. Marshal Tetford ignored the request, and detached a dark, quiet man who looked like a 'breed Indian, to ride ahead and quarter for sign.

Lew's impression of Marshal Tetford was based on what he had observed so far. Tetford was made of iron and had a ramrod up his back. It was hard to imagine him ever deviating from his duty. But he was not all that hard, because an hour down-country he angled to ride with Lew and said, 'How many crates of carbines did you say?' and when Lew told him, the federal officer wagged his head. 'The marshal's office up in Denver got information about someone buying new Winchesters by the hundreds, plus ammunition. The rumour was that they were being peddled to Mex *pronunciados* down at the border, but no one down there knew anythin' about Messicans taking delivery down there.' Tetford squinted ahead against the rising sun-smash. 'We didn't know . . . This morning over where we caught you boys, the more I listened, the more it looked like I'd stumbled onto something no one expected.'

118

Lew asked a question. 'You were after the men who stole that money pouch and killed those two men on the stagecoach?'

'Yeah. It's an army payroll. There's riders tracking those raiders coming north from the town of Seward, a couple hunnert miles from here. I was already down at Saint George when the telegram arrived for me to get up a deputised posse and head down this way to cut them off, if they were going north.'

Tetford studied Lew, Reg and Tom, and his lips pulled back in something very close to an expression of hard amusement. 'I guess hitting me last night was understandable—but I'll remember it.'

One of the possemen riding back in thin dust, halloed and pointed. A solitary horseman was loping in their direction from the south.

It was the 'breed. He drew rein, slackened his gait and when the marshal came up he said, 'Dust. Lots of it.' He twisted to gesture. 'Down near that bluff a few miles.' As he sat forward and lowered his arm, the 'breed also said, 'I guess they was tellin' the truth. There's a hell of a lot of fresh sign west of here, like a lot of riders come up, then turned back. It's too far so I didn't follow it. But sure as hell there's someone down there, and somethin' is going on.'

Marshal Tetford solemnly rolled and lit a smoke, narrowed, pale eyes studying the onward open country. It was obvious to Lew that he did not like having so much open country to cross. Finally, he started forward again, at a dead walk, trailing bluish smoke in the still air.

Once he turned toward Lew and said, 'How many?'

'Damned close to twenty Mexicans, Bill Smith and his three partners, Slim, Sam, and Joe. Joe looks like he's maybe half or two-thirds Mexican.'

Tetford had another question. 'That Gatling gun—it's in a crate?'

'Was last night. That's all I can tell you, Marshal.'

As they rode onward Lee began to think about that Gatling gun. The more he thought about it, the less he liked what he was thinking. But if they were loading the pack animals—no doubt doing it in a hurry this morning—they would not uncrate the Gatling gun. Still, just the idea of such a weapon under these conditions was enough to make a man's hair stand up.

He did not like the odds either, or the fact that he and his partners were still unarmed. In fact he did not like much of anything about his present condition, but of one thing he was certain: Marshal Will Tetford would not allow Lew and his partners to depart.

Tetford aimed for a sandstone bluff and halted in its meagre shade while he sent the 'breed and the bandy-legged older man to scout.

While waiting, Marshal Tetford got down and opened a tin of peaches with a boot-knife, drank the syrup then, using his knife, speared peach-halves and ate them.

The other possemen did the same. That slightly stooped rider who had tossed Lew his tinned milk, handed around three tins of peaches, ignored the thanks he got, and everyone ate in silence.

When they were finished Tetford said, 'Milt; it's like old times.'

The weathered, sinewy man called Milt answered as though he had been doing a lot of thinking lately. 'Yeah, like old times ... Captain, when you come by the ranch to visit, I told myself I never yet seen you, that something didn't happen ... You know where I ought to be right now?'

Marshal Tetford nodded his head. 'Back near the meadows cleaning springs or hunting varmints, or branding baby calves. I'm glad you're not, Milt. You were the best sergeant in the outfit.'

Milt did not seem elated by the compliment. He found a plug and ripped off a cud with strong teeth, studying Tetford with sceptical eyes. 'Captain, we're both gettin' a little long in the tooth for this sort of thing.'

Tetford agreed with a nod, then strolled away from the shade and stood out yonder looking southward for a long time. Before he returned

121

Reg and Milt got into a quiet conversation. Marshal Tetford had been a Union officer back during the war, and Milt Downey had been a sergeant in Tetford's horse-company. Tetford had been a good tactical officer, Milt told Reg. One of the best. When everyone else was losing men like flies at Gettysburg, Tetford flanked a regiment of Confederates and broke them, scattering foot soldiers like chaff without losing a man.

But Milt and the other possemen had also heard the Gatling gun mentioned. They asked Reg and Tom about it. The answers they got were encouraging, but that was all. Every one of Tetford's riders knew about Gatling guns.

By the time the marshal walked over, hands clasped in back, head down in thought, the men were ready to move, and the horses had been rested. Will Tetford halted, gazing at the mustangers. He raised a hand to stroke his jaw where Lew had hit him last night. Then he said, 'We don't have any spare weapons, gents ... My scouts are returning ... I don't like the idea of the odds, and I like it even less that you three are unarmed ... Any suggestions?'

Tom had one. 'I never done any soldiering, Marshal, but I've done my share of riding in country like this ... Them bastards would give their eye teeth to catch us three ... We could sort of sashay down in that direction, let 'em see us, then lose 'em in the rocks and brush and all.'

Reg and Lew turned to stare in horror at the grinning big red-faced Mormon. Reg Bentley looked as though he was going to choke.

Marshal Tetford gazed at Tom Lee from an expressionless face before speaking. 'If we had a dozen more men, I'd say chance it. Right now, the way men get beaten under these circumstances, is to split up.'

That ended the discussion because the scouts rode up in a stiff jog, stepped off and led their animals into shade before reporting. The bandy-legged man wagged his head. 'Looks like a blessed army, Marshal. They got a wagon hitched up, a few head of loose-stock, a big string of Mex pack mules about ready to start out, and hell, they out-number us pretty bad.' As he paused, looking steadily at the federal officer as though expecting a comment, the bandy-legged man shrugged thick shoulders. When Tetford did not speak, the bandy-legged man also said, 'They're in a hell of a hurry. Most likely they can't travel fast, none of them, the Messicans with their laden mules nor the other fellers with their wagon, and they figure those three gents are high-tailing it up to Saint George to get the law after them.'

Tetford finally spoke. 'That's about the size of it.' His blue gaze remained fixed upon the shorter man. 'Anything else?'

'Yeah. One thing. They know about those three gents being down here—but they don't know about us being down here, nor about the posse coming up from Seward.'

Marshal Tetford got that near-smile down around his lips again. It put Lew Palmer in mind of a school teacher showing approval when some child came up with the right answer to a complicated question.

Tetford then said, 'How is the country down there?'

This time the 'breed answered. 'They're on the east side of a big barranca. We got to keep to the west of it, and raise no dust. Unless they get worried and commence scouting around, we can get down on the far side of that barranca . . . Surprise 'em.'

Tetford nodded gently. 'We'd better surprise them, Jim.' He added nothing more to that. He did not have to. They totalled nine riders, three of whom did not have guns. The men they were after totalled either twenty-four or twenty-five—armed to the teeth.

Tetford looked around. The men were sitting in shade as silent and motionless as stones, looking back at him. He said, 'Jim, head out. Find us a good way to flank them. We'll follow along.'

The 'breed was mounting when the other possemen arose dusting their britches. The former sergeant called Milt snugged up his cincha, looking across saddle leather. 'I wonder how long a man's luck lasts?' he asked quietly, of no one in particular.

Will Tetford got astride, evened up his reins, looked back just once, and started riding. Lew, Reg and Tom were in the bunched-up press of horsemen who followed him out of the shade.

It was hot. Under these circumstances it was impossible not to raise dust, but riding at a walk did not raise much, nor scuff it very high off the ground.

The 'breed was small in the distance, riding westerly. Even if he was seen it probably would not arouse Bill Smith very much. One man riding away from the wagon-camp posed no immediate threat.

It seemed an eternity before they had the rear of the barranca on their left. They no longer had the 'breed in sight, probably because he was now riding due east in order to get close to the rear of the barranca, and there was quite a bit of underbrush over there.

They halted once when Tom raised an arm. A high, large banner of dust was moving swiftly southward a mile or two east of the wagon-camp. They lost sight of it when it passed across the far side of the barranca.

Tom said, 'Them danged mustangs again.'

No one questioned his judgment as they started forward again. Lew was sure the renegades had also seen that cloud of dust, because it was in front of them, while they watched it they would have their backs to the barranca.

Jim appeared on foot. He had been watching the posse's approach from the shelter of a big old bedraggled thorn-pin bush. There was no sign of his horse.

Will Tetford looked back, wearing that near-smile again. They had managed to get behind the barranca without arousing the men working furiously around in front of it. It seemed to Lew that Marshal Tetford deserved less commendation for this accomplishment, than those racing mustangs which had diverted the renegades long enough for the possemen to accomplish their purpose.

Now, the heat was making a blue haze in the distance, and up closer it created slowly undulating waves a few feet above the ground. It was actually not full summertime yet, but evidently the Wolf Hole country either did not know that, or functioned according to its own set of rules.

They dismounted in underbrush, sweating profusely, and Jim showed them where to tie their horses in some thin shade among stands of more dusty underbrush.

Marshal Tetford stood like a statue, silently looking, and listening. It was possible to occasionally hear sounds from around in front of the barranca, but because the sandstone bluff was thickly massive, such noises had to be loud to be heard behind it.

He raised his hat for cool air to waft through his hair. He used a blue bandana to mop off sweat, and when the possemen all returned, carrying Winchesters except for Reg, Lew and Tom, the marshal seemed pleased, although it was hard to tell with a man like William Tetford, exactly what his feelings were.

But he showed that faint, almost indiscernible lift at the outer corners of his wide mouth which seemed to presage a smile, and he said, 'Milt, there's a good brush cover along the north side. Take three men ... I'll bring the others in support, but we'll go higher up and around the slope.'

Milt looked, frowned, and said, 'You got no cover up there, Marshal.'

Lee and his partners had already made this same stalk. Granted, they had done it in the darkness when protective cover had not been as critical as it was now, but they had done it, and that mattered, so Lew spoke up.

'Marshal, my partners and I can lead you around the lower flank to some pretty thick underbrush at the north end of the hillside ... Milt will be south of us. We'll all be hidden that way.'

Tetford's features were expressionless. He listened but did not look at the man who had spoken for a while. Finally, though, he said, 'You know the way?' and when Lee assured him that all three of them knew the way, he nodded

127

at Milt. 'You stay close, then, Milt, in the brush, and give us time to get north of you . . . When we're in position I'll fire the first shot.'

Milt shook sweat off his chin and turned to select the men he wanted with him. Just before he led them away, that bandy-legged, older man tossed something to Lew Palmer, and grinned. 'You got to shove it down a man's throat for it to be accurate, but it's better than rocks.'

Lew looked at the little big-bored under-and-over .41 calibre Derringer he had caught. Evidently the bandy-legged man carried it as his hide-out weapon. Evidently too, he did not like the idea of Lew facing what they all did not doubt would be a battle, without at least something to shoot.

Tetford looked at the men standing with him, then jerked his head and started forward, motioning for Lew to get in front and lead the way.

CHAPTER THIRTEEN

SMOKE, DUST AND BLOOD

Tom and Reg were close to Lew when the big Mormon spoke approvingly of Marshal Tetford. 'Sure knows his business, don't he? Stands straight like old Gen'l Grant and all.'

Reg looked sourly at Tom Lee. 'Soldiers never inspired me very much. Especially his kind.'

They had no time for a further discussion of Marshal Tetford. They were taken into underbrush which had an acidy smell during the hot days, which it did not seem to possess at night.

There was no sign of Milt or his companions. A braying mule broke the silence, and several men shouted in Spanish. Lew assumed the mule had got pinched by some part of his pack and was letting the world know about it. He welcomed this interlude as he had welcomed the earlier one when the band of mustangs had run past.

The posseman directly in front, who was crouching so low his carbine was only inches from the ground, suddenly halted, slowly sank down, and seemed to freeze. The men behind him took their cue from this, and without having any idea what had motivated the man ahead, they also sank down and stopped moving.

Two Mexicans were coming into the brush, talking casually as they advanced. By the time Lew could see them, head and shoulders high over the scrub, they were only scant yards from Tetford and the possemen up front with him. Lew watched the rigid figure directly in front very slowly put aside its Winchester, draw its handgun, tip up the barrel, and wait.

Tetford abruptly arose like a *fantasma* out of the earth, or so it seemed to the *arrieros*, aimed his weapon at them and gave a harsh order in border-Spanish, the language of these Mexicans.

They were too paralysed for a couple of seconds to obey. Behind the federal lawman one posseman arose, then another, and finally, the three mustangers also arose, without arms, but adding to the numbers. Two sets of muddy dark eyes moved slowly past, around, then back to the gun in Tetford's hand, then each *arriero* lifted out his sixgun and let it fall. Each man had a sheath-knife too, but Tetford ignored them as he gave another curt order. This time the Mexicans noticeably quailed. The order had been for them to face around with their backs to Marshal Tetford. In their country this order commonly was followed by the order to run. The men with guns then practised marksmanship. One Mexican spoke breathlessly, 'Señor, we will help you.'

Tetford repeated his command, more harshly the second time, and as the terrified *arrieros* began to turn, Tetford stepped ahead and struck hard twice with his gunbarrel. He then stepped over the bodies and paused to glance back as he said, 'You boys take their guns.' Tom and Reg each acquired a sixgun. As Lew passed the bodies he saw blood being absorbed into the powdery soil as fast as it dripped.

Reg was the last man to pass and he did not know whether the *arrieros* were dead or not, but he did not like the idea of having Mexicans with knives behind him, so he yanked loose their belts and hurriedly and roughly bound them both.

When Lew saw Tetford fade from sight up ahead, he also got lower in the underbrush, and slightly behind him Tom said, 'They're gettin' ready to pull out. Look yonder.'

Lew's retort was curt. 'Get your damned head down.'

Now, although they could not see ahead, they could smell animals in the dust and heat. They could also hear sentences in two languages, and profanity which was a mixture of both.

Lee sweated and examined the weapon in his hand. It was about as useless as teats on a man, but, as the bandy-legged man had said, it was a little better than just throwing rocks.

A man whistled loudly. Other men called back and forth. Lew's curiosity got the best of him. He arose inches at a time until he could see what Tetford and the posseman lying up ahead beside him were watching.

Six grunting men were trying to get that Gatling gun crate balanced evenly on a large, muscular mare-mule. There was more than one crate, but they did not weigh the same, therefore the sweating and swearing packers had to juggle the load, striving for an even weight on both sides. It was taking more time than the Mexican colonel liked. He swore at the packers and went over to assist. Lew watched him with fascination. This was the first time he had seen the Mexican officer since they had been his prisoners.

Bill Smith and the thickly oaken man called Joe walked into sight. Lew watched them too. They were only slightly farther away than a man could threw a stone. They were also unsuspecting, and perfect targets.

Reg arose on Lew's far side to scowl and say, 'What is Tetford waiting for?'

As though that were a cue, the first gunshot sounded, and for the length of time it would take to blink an eye, those completely surprised packers dropped their hands to watch the Mexican colonel crumple slowly to the ground.

Then all hell broke loose and Lew had no time to reflect upon the accuracy of Marshal Tetford's back-shot.

To the south of them guns thundered from the underbrush where Milt and his posseman had been waiting. Tom and Reg shouldered Lew aside to rush ahead, up where a posseman was standing in full view, Winchester to his shoulder, firing with the singleness of purpose of a man in a shooting gallery.

Men cried out, dropped lead shanks allowing terrified mules with full packs to break away in all directions, running for their lives. Both the harness animals on the wagon tongue reared and fought to break their tie-ropes. Panic, like terror, was contagious among animals. Even the calmest of the mules and horses hurled themselves backwards to gain freedom, and those which had not been tied charged through the routed *arrieros*, bowling a few over and further scattering the others.

The moment of surprise lasted no more than four or five seconds, but while it lasted Bill Smith's crew had little protection. Finally, the moment passed and a withering, if inaccurate return-fire brisked up, gunsmoke hazed the still, hot atmosphere, and men shouting to one another sounded more defiant and challenging now.

Two simultaneous slugs cutting limbs from the underbrush in either side of that pot-shooter who was standing erect and exposed, brought the man to his senses. He dropped to the ground.

Reg and Tom were prone, up near Marshal Tetford, thoroughly concealed by underbrush, which also hampered their visibility. Neither of them wasted a shot. Neither of them was by nature subject to agitation nor excitability.

Lew did not creep up there until the posseman with the carbine sat up to re-load, saw Lew with his little Derringer, and tossed his sixgun over with a sweaty and red-faced grin, then the posseman too began crawling.

Lew had difficulty seeing once he got up into the prone skirmish line Marshal Tetford had formed. Dust was as thick as a cloud. He counted four bodies, two on their faces, two on their backs. He also saw the carbines and belt-guns lying beside the carcasses.

Finally, those team animals broke free and despite the howling admonitions of someone Lew thought was probably Bill Smith, no one ran out into plain sight to try and spring onto the wagon-seat to set the binders and grab the lines.

Lew was fascinated at the way the runaway team carried that heavily-laden wagon over boulders, across the tops of brush clumps, and kept it rocking first on one side then the other side as it careened wildly southward.

Finally, a wheel struck a huge and immovable boulder head-on. Spokes flew, felloes shattered, a steel tyre crumpled, and the wagon was dragged another ten yards with its axle ploughing a furrow, before the horses could drag it no farther.

Tetford made a curt gesture and led his possemen farther northward, to the very edge of the underbrush. The noise of gunfire made it impossible to be heard, so he conveyed his thoughts with more hand signals. They were easy to understand. Lew guessed they were probably military hand and arm commands.

Tetford had his men strung out beneath underbrush again, and took his time aligning them. Back where they had been concealed, the desperate renegades were methodically shredding thorn-pin bushes. Out where they were lying now, not a single shot came in their direction.

Milt had also moved, but Milt had started shifting position shortly after the fight had started. He seemed to be of the opinion that men who fired, then rolled and fired again, then rolled again, did not make very good targets.

Marshal Tetford's other reason for crawling northward instead of down where Milt was, so that they could join up, was obvious the moment Lew leaned from beneath a big bush and looked southward. Up until now, they had been unable to see along the front of the barranca where the wagon had been tied, and where a number of men were pressing back out of sight to avoid being shot.

He could see those men. He even recognised Bill Smith and the dark, muscular man called Joe. They were looking northward, carbines held in both hands up across their bodies, neither firing nor taking part in the fight. Neither were the five or six other men down there with them.

Lee watched Marshal Tetford easing around in the underbrush using his carbine to push limbs away which were armed with inch-long thorns. Tetford was deliberately angling so as to be able to shoot into the band of men in front of the barranca who were trapped there unable to move in any direction without exposing themselves.

Reg and Tom were not that systematic. As soon as they saw Bill Smith and his companions, they took long rests, elbows planted firmly on the ground, and fired one bullet each.

A large *arriero* went drunkenly into the cliff-face at his back, then slid down it and rolled to one side. Smith and the others did not waste a second now. They knew that someone was finally in a position to reach them. They fell to the ground and fired into the northerly underbrush, but high, and in a scything manner. There was too much gunsmoke now to tell where an individual gust of it came from. In fact it was getting difficult now to even see those men along the front of the barranca.

Across the way, eastward, there was no shelter except for that one stand of scrub Tom Lee had used yesterday to affect the capture of the men riding with Smith. Otherwise, the country was open. Two *arrieros* suddenly burst out of that underbrush fleeing eastward. Neither man had burdened himself with his carbine. They were both very fast, and they were also knowledgeable. They zig-zagged as they ran. Lew did not fire. The distance was too great for a sixgun, and he did not particularly

136

want to shoot them anyway.

But other men did. Little spurts of grey dust and ancient dirt sprang into the air around the Mexicans. Neither was hit and each seemed to increase his speed as he constantly altered course.

Tom Lee looked up at Lew, face red as a beet and dripping sweat. He was laughing.

Marshal Tetford arose to one knee, took an arm rest, followed the distant men through the sights of his Winchester, and Reg suddenly bumped him. Then looked embarrassed as he apologised.

Marshal Tetford's cold blue gaze rested for a moment upon Bentley, then was distracted as some men down along the front of the barranca-wall began shouting. They were no longer using their weapons and they shouted louder as the gunfire began to diminish.

Lew knew it was over before the last shot was fired. Evidently so did the infinitely more experienced U.S. Marshal. He did not stand up in sight, but he grounded the Winchester and leaned on it gazing over the area where dead men lay amid scattered camp equipment and horse gear.

In ways, the abrupt silence was louder than the gunfire had been. Lew watched a dishevelled *arriero* get painfully to his feet from an indentation in the ground. He was holding a carbine loosely above his head. He was a short, thick, unwashed-looking individual and when he called out it was not in English to say 'I surrender' or 'I give up', it was in Spanish to say, 'It is enough.'

Everyone waited, the men lying under a fiercely hot sun in other little swales, the men down in front of the barranca, the wounded who were either moaning or were unwilling to moan, the concealed men in the underbrush, even the other men here and there who emulated the dishevelled Mexican by also standing up in plain sight with guns above their heads.

Lew watched Marshal Tetford. He did not move, did not make a sound, and did not change expression. His cold blue eyes went from man to man out there. He watched the smoke lift enough so that he could see the bodies. And, finally, he pushed up to his feet and stepped out of the northward underbrush, aware that every eye was fixed on him.

Reg came over beside Lew and Tom, looking pained as he watched, but he kept his thoughts to himself. This was Marshal Tetford's dramatic moment and he was playing the part to the hilt. Lew glanced northward, looking for Milt, wondering whether Milt had seen Will Tetford do this during the war, perhaps when he had surprised and captured Confederates.

Reg could hold it back no longer when he growled to his companions, 'Who the hell does he think he is, Julius Caesar? Look at those

138

filthy, greasy bastards out there. Look at this damned desolate country. Don't look like Rome to me.'

Lew said nothing as he watched, but Tom was smiling. He was fascinated by Tetford's slow pacing down to face the men along the cliff-face. Tom had never seen anything like it. After a while he said, 'Julius Caesar wore a skirt. I've seen pictures of him. Marshal Tetford is more like—well—maybe Gen'l Grant or somebody.'

Tetford stopped about three or four yards from the motionless men in front of the cliff-face, looked at them a long time, then snarled,

'Walk out here and pile your guns! Every damned one of you!' As he was being obeyed, he looked to his right and called, 'Milt! Total our casualties. The rest of you possemen come along, find shovels, and start digging graves and rounding up the wounded.'

Tom was thrilled. 'He sure knows what to say, don't he? Look at them Messicans straggling over to toss their weapons at his feet.'

Reg looked around at the big Mormon, stared a long time, did not say a word, and caught Lew's eye as he disgustedly began to shake his head.

CHAPTER FOURTEEN

RETURN TO THE HORSE CAMP

When Bill Smith saw Lew and his partners, he stared at them a long time in stony silence, then turned his back. That muscular dark man called Joe reacted a little differently. He actually smiled at Lew, Reg and Tom Lee. It was a thin, bitter smile tinged with admiration, and when no one else came near the horse-hunters, in fact avoided them, Joe returned from throwing his weapons on the heap and said, 'I'll tell you what I think. You fellers got a lot more guts than brains.'

Reg was hostile. 'It's the other way around. You fellers are the damned idiots.'

Joe shrugged thick shoulders. Around them the prisoners were being herded together. Reluctant or surly ones were hastened along with rough handling from Milt and the other possemen.

Marshal Tetford strolled down where the wagon was stranded. He was down there a long while, and when he returned, looking grave and thoughtful, he took Lew aside and said, 'That's it. That's part of the loot the Mexican government's been accusing us of stealing. I never expected anything like this. Incidentally, did you know Bill Smith is Wade Hampton?' At Lew's blank look Tetford said, 'You didn't? Well, Hampton's got warrants out on him from California to Washington. He's not only a gun-runner, he's also a notorious criminal and killer. The rewards must total about five or six thousand dollars.'

Lew's eyes widened. Tetford's cold blue eyes kindled a little. He slapped Lew lightly on the shoulder. 'Maybe comin' down here after wild horses was the best thing you ever did, Mister Palmer.' He walked up where his men had two injured Mexicans and four dead ones, stood wide-legged, hands clasped behind his back, staring. He did not say a word, just stared, then went over where Bill Smith was being guarded with Joe, Slim and Sam, and did the same thing, stood with both hands behind him regarding the renegades. But this time he spoke.

'We're going to wait here for the posse coming up your back-trail. They want you for the murder of those two stagers.'

Smith scowled. 'We didn't kill those men. We didn't even know the Mexicans had stopped a coach until that dead one over there brought in the money pouch.'

Tetford was unimpressed. 'And of course you didn't know they'd been murdering churchmen down in Mexico when they stole all that gold and whatnot. And you didn't know you violated federal law, selling them guns and ammunition.'

Bill Smith brought out his plug and bit off a corner. He did not say another word as he cheeked his cud and gazed at the federal lawman.

Tetford's stare did not waver as it went from man to man, and returned to Bill Smith. 'You boys will go up to Saint George with me. The Seward posse can have the Mexicans.'

Smith turned aside to expectorate before turning back to say, 'We'd rather go south with the possemen.'

Tetford's hard gaze showed a sardonic, cruel light. 'No you wouldn't, Mister Hampton. Those are civilian possemen and they're out for blood. I've been a lawman a long time. I've seen civilian posses start out with live prisoners many times, and arrive at their destination with dead ones.'

Smith's eyes wavered. He said, 'We'll go north with you.'

Milt came over to interrupt. 'We got no casualties, Captain. The Messicans got four dead, two wounded, and a couple more hurt a little when those mules stampeded over the top of them.'

'Burial details out, Milt?'

'Yes, sir.'

'Send a couple of men out to round up the mules and bring them back. We'll camp here until the Seward posse arrives. There's grub in the wagon ... Look inside when you go down there. You'll likely never again see so much loot if you live to be a hundred . . . Have a couple of the boys take that team off the wagon; have all the animals watered and turned out.'

Milt nodded, gazing past. 'Which one of them is Hampton?'

Tetford jerked a thumb. 'That one.'

While Milt was staring at Bill Smith Reg found his horsehide coat, and although it was far too hot to wear it, he had it hooked over one arm as he went in search of the weapons he and his partners had lost.

Lew went over to him, suggested they go after their animals, and walked back through the underbrush. As they walked Lew told his partner who Bill Smith was. Then he mentioned the bounty money and Reg stopped in his tracks.

'How much?'

'Around five or six thousand dollars. That's Tetford's guess.'

Reg gazed past his partner, back in the direction of the camp. 'Damned near two thousand dollars each. I never had that much. I never even seen that much money. Did Tetford say him and his crew come in for a share?'

'No, he didn't say. But I know for a fact he can't accept any. Federal lawmen are prohibited from taking rewards.'

'How about Milt and the others?'

'I don't know, but I'd guess it's ours because

we showed them where those bastards were and sort of led them down here, and helped 'em make the round-up . . . Let's get the horses.'

By the time they had returned with three saddle animals Tom had gone with Milt to take the harness horses off the tongue, and to also look inside the wagon. He was still awed when Reg and Lew found him over by the fire-ring where possemen were preparing a meal from supplies taken from the renegades.

Tom said, 'That feller Milt figures there's got to be maybe as much as sixty, seventy thousand dollars worth of loot in them boxes in the wagon. I never saw anythin' like it. Why didn't the Messican government get up an army and come after it?'

'Because right now the Mex government is fightin' for its life against rebels Bill Smith has been arming. Anyway, it'll go back.' He then told Tom what he had recently told Reg about the reward on Bill Smith, and after Tom Lee had digested that, he made a practical comment which had not as yet occurred to either of his companions. 'Sure as hell those other bastards, Joe, Slim and Sam, will have bounties on them too.'

Lew thought about that, and would have gone over to verify it, except that Marshal Tetford was supervising the sweating possemen who were tying their prisoners. It would not have been a good time to divert him.

The sun was dropping behind the barranca by the time mounted possemen brought in the pack animals, which were off-loaded, and Tetford prised open two crates on the ground and left them open for his men to see the illegal guns, then he also opened one of the Gatling gun crates to expose its contents too, and the possemen stood in silence for a while, then went over to the fire-ring to eat.

Over there, the 'breed called Jim was heaping a tin plate when he said, 'Gun like that will stop wars.'

Several men grunted agreement with him.

Marshal Tetford came over to hunker and fill a plate. For a while everyone ate in silence. Hunger, which had not bothered them until now, turned out to have been there all the time, but water was what they had wanted most after the fight. A peculiarity about combat was that it left men inordinately thirsty, even when they had not fought under a blazing sun.

Tetford put down his tin plate and reached for a cup of black java. 'Jim, when you're through, scout down their back-trail. Somewhere down there is a posse. I'd like to know how long we got to stay here before it arrives.'

The bandy-legged man came over to hunker beside Lew, and grin. Lew fished forth the .41 calibre Derringer and handed it over with a smile. He had not fired it. The bandy-legged man pocketed his little gun and said, 'I never been in a battle before. Have you?'

Lew hadn't. 'Never have and never wanted to.'

The older man laughed. 'It turned out all right.'

It had indeed turned out all right, but as the day lengthened and reaction set in, Lew went in search of a canteen, drank deeply, and finally began to feel his stomach rolling and his nerves crawling.

The dead had been carried away to the shallow pits Tetford's possemen had scratched in the flinty soil. The prisoners were being fed, after their conquerors had eaten, and Bill Smith was sitting on a saddle on the ground, facing Marshal Tetford. They seemed to be conversing calmly, detachedly.

It was dark when the 'breed rode back into camp and cared for his horse before approaching the federal officer. He had seen dust on the back-trail of the border-jumpers, but it had been so distant all he'd been able to make out was that it was being made by a band of horsemen heading toward the camp. He thought they would probably arrive long after dark—if they did not halt to camp for the night— otherwise, if it was indeed the Seward possemen, they would ride in tomorrow morning.

Marshal Tetford was satisfied. He could think

146

of no reason for any other horsemen to be tracking the Mexicans. Neither could he imagine any reason for a travelling band of riders to be crossing this empty, desolate and uninhabited area, so as he arose to leave Bill Smith, he said, 'Jim, you and I'll ride down to their camp.'

Smith cocked a sceptical eye. 'Marshal, you don't have to do that. Tomorrow will be soon enough. It'll be a long ride in the night and you've earned a rest.'

Jim and Will Tetford looked at the seated renegade. Smith was relaxed, calm, and calculating. He said to Jim: 'Go saddle the marshal's horse,' and as the 'breed walked away—not toward the hobbled horses grazing beyond camp, but toward the fire-ring where men were still eating—Bill Smith's perpetually narrowed eyes were nearly hidden as he smiled slightly.

'There's more bullion in my wagon than five men could cash in and live off for the rest of their lives—live high and mighty, Marshal.'

Tetford's expression did not change as he returned the renegade's gaze. After a moment he turned on his heel without a word and walked out where the horses were grazing, and Jim, who saw him heading out there, jumped up from the fire-ring and hurried out there too.

Milt strolled over where the mustangers were sifting through captured bedrolls for the three

147

cleanest. After Tetford's departure he was in charge of the possemen. He watched the horse-hunters make their selection, then dryly said, 'You boys did right well.'

No one commented. The bedrolls were old, dirty, smelly and ragged—and those were the best ones.

Milt spoke again. 'I was talkin' to Joe, that half-Mex lookin' ape. He said Slim and Sam are wanted for bank robbery in Texas. Two thousand dollars on each of them.'

Reg looked up. 'What about Joe; he's downright virtuous?'

Milt smiled. 'Funny thing about Joe, when I asked, he just leaned there grinning at me . . . Yeah, I'd say there's money on him somewhere. Cap Tetford will find out. One thing he's real good at is running them down and finding out all about them . . . We talked, Cap and me . . . Federal lawmen can't get a cut in on rewards. I expect maybe that's because the government don't want to end up having a whole agency of bounty hunters. Anyway, he says Hampton's bounty goes to you fellers for showin' him how to recover the Seward money pouch, and for leadin' us down here.'

Lew and Reg were standing up now, looking at Milt. Tom, who never anticipated a round-about approach to a subject because he was completely without guile, went on examining his appropriated bedroll.

'Well,' Milt said, shifting position a little as though he were uncomfortable, 'thing my friends been wondering is . . .'

Lew lent some assistance. 'Whether me and my partners would be satisfied with the bounty money on Smith—Hampton; whatever his name is—and leave the other rewards to you fellers.'

Milt nodded his head, smiling a little.

Lew and Reg exchanged a glance. Reg shrugged. They both turned toward Tom, who had finally shaken out the Mexican bedroll. Without even looking up Tom demonstrated that he had been listening to every word. 'Fine with me, if it's all right with you two.' He then started dragging the Mexican bedroll away seeking a place to bed down.

Lew nodded and Milt hovered a short while longer until he could decently return to the hunkered, silent, waiting men over the the little fire where a coffee pot was heating.

When full darkness arrived there was no moon, and even when it would arrive hours later, it would no longer be full. But the night remained warm as Milt and the other possemen went over to examine the bindings of the prisoners, and to start the night-long watch, in relays which Milt organised.

Lew and Reg took their appropriated bedrolls out where Tom had settled, spread them and sat down to shuck gunbelts, hats and boots. Reg examined his injured toe. The swelling had completely subsided although the sprained joint was still painful, even to the touch. He tossed his hat aside, eased back looking straight up, and said, 'I've decided that hunting wild horses isn't it, either ... Stone masoning and mustanging ... Lew, what else is there?'

From the nearby darkness Lew's reply was quietly drowsy. 'Back to range riding.'

But Reg demurred. 'Naw; remember us crawling out of that little door above the front door of that house up in Colorado and walking on snowshoes to the barn that winter we hired on to feed cattle?'

Lew remembered. 'Yeah. Being snowed-in was bad enough. Feeding cattle off a big old rack through three feet of snow was worse. But what griped my butt was you winning all my money and my spurs before a thaw set in.'

'What else could we do but stay inside and play poker all winter? Besides, I gave back the spurs.'

Reg laughed, then said, 'No stone work, no more wild-horse hunting, and no more cowboying.'

Lew was trying to sleep. 'We could buy a saloon with bounty money. Saloon-keepers don't have to go outside during winter, they stay dry and warm and get lots of company. And they make money ... Now shut up I'm trying to sleep.'

Reg ignored the admonition. 'How about

goin' out to California and gettin' into the land business?'

'... The what?'

'You heard 'em talking at the poolhall in Kremling about how land dealers out in California are makin' money hand over fist peddlin' to the easterners who are flocking out there.'

'What in the hell do we know about peddling land, Reg?'

'We've rode over a lot of it. What do you have to know?'

'Go to sleep.'

'Lew...?'

'In a minute I'm coming up off this bedroll and stamp the crap out of your busted toe if you don't shut up!'

Tom, who had been listening, giggled, and Reg let go with a big sigh and remained silent, but he did not sleep for a long while.

Everyone else excepting the guards seemed to sleep well, and the guards probably would have if they had dared to.

By dawn, when the chill had set in, Tom Lee went over and joined Milt at the stone-ring to get a fire going. By grey pre-dawn they looked slightly less than human, and although good-natured Tom Lee was willing to talk and be friendly, Milt was not, and would not be until he had tanked up on black coffee.

The camp stirred to life. Mostly, the men had

151

little to say. Once, when Bill Smith called Milt over and mentioned the treasure in the wagon, Milt pointed a thick finger and said, 'One more word and I'm going to break your jaw.'

Smith remained silent.

The *arrieros* were hungry. Milt's possemen were too, and took their time at preparing breakfast and eating it, before taking food to the prisoners. Sam and Slim, who had said almost nothing since the night before, eyed Reg and Lew as they went past, and Sam said, 'Cowboy, damned good thing it happened your way, because I was comin' after you.'

Reg looked down, spat into the churned dust in front of Sam, and limped on his way.

The sun was climbing, heat was on the way, visibility had not yet been impaired by heat-haze, and one of the possemen, down guarding the broken wagon, sang out and gestured with his carbine.

A party of riders was approaching through the newday brilliance. The camp went completely silent while all eyes turned to watch. Marshal Tetford was riding ahead with a heavy-jawed, small-eyed, lanky man who wore an expression which had been blasted out of pure granite. He was wearing a dull little lawman's star on his vest, and as the party passed the wagon and rode into the camp, the hard-faced man reined to a halt, looked around, swung to the ground as his riders were doing, and walked over where the

Mexican prisoners were eyeing him without moving. He spoke harshly in fluent Spanish. He asked that the men who had stolen the payroll, killed the stage-driver and gunguard, and had then destroyed the stage be pointed out to him.

No one moved. Several Mexicans looked at the ground, and none of them made a sound. The sheriff glanced over his shoulder where Marshal Tetford and the other recently-arrived possemen were getting coffee at the fire-ring, with their backs purposeful towards the prisoners and their interrogator. It almost seemed as though this had been planned.

It had. The sheriff faced forward. In a quiet, deadly tone of voice he spoke in Spanish again. 'Look you, men. The federal men are going north with the *norteamericano prisoneros*. You are all going south with me, to the place where you killed those men and left their widows and children to cry. It is a very long ride. I think not all of you will survive such a long ride. Maybe none of you will survive it, for to escape permits my riders and me to shoot you . . . Point out to me which are the men I seek.'

The Mexicans glanced back and forth. This was something they understood because it was also their custom, except that below the border they all would have been told to run for it, and would have been killed from behind as they fled.

That thin, nervous Mexican who had

153

interrupted when the ugly Mexican had wanted to knife-fight Tom Lee, raised his head defiantly and, avoiding the glances of his companions, pointed. 'It was those three hombres, *jefe*. Sandoval, Iturbide and Bohorquez.'

After that the silence returned. During it could be heard the quiet discussions going on over at the fire-ring where preparations to depart were under way.

The sheriff studied three particular Mexicans a long while as though fixing their faces in his mind, then he turned on his heel. Behind him, the three murderers turned on the thin man. He wilted a little under their threats and curses but remained resolute, and when the tirade ended he said, 'The colonel told all of us not to go near a town nor a roadway. To do nothing like you did. Are you deaf? Didn't you hear what the *jefe* said? The rest of us should not have to die because of you who are fools.'

Mostly, the other prisoners stared at the ground and were silent. It could reasonably be assumed that they agreed with the thin man, but none of them said so.

Lew, Reg and Tom left their Mexican blankets where they were and went in search of enough water to wash in. By the time they were ready to eat, Tetford's riders and the newcomers from down near the town of Seward in Arizona, were briskly getting the mules ready to be

154

packed.

The camp was a busy place. Lew, Reg and Tom were already being excluded from the activity. They would have helped but there were more than enough other men for everything that had to be done. Tom wondered about something. 'They can't move that wagon on three wheels. You expect they'll come back for the loot?'

Lew looked pained at such a question, but Reg, who had been down to the wagon several times, went right on eating as he said, 'They won't have to. Even Bill Smith wasn't ignorant enough to bring a rig up here a hundred miles from a blacksmith shop without a spare. There's a wheel chained underneath the bed of the wagon.'

Tom was impressed. 'By golly, he sure thought of everything, didn't he?'

Reg raised his head to watch the Seward lawman yank Bill Smith to his feet, whirl him, and put steel cuffs on Smith's wrists in back. 'Almost everything.' Reg said, and drained his tin cup.

Marshal Tetford strolled over. He had shaved and washed, the only man in camp who had used a razor. There was enough water, but shaving, even washing, had not been uppermost in many minds this morning.

Tetford hunkered down and got right to the point. 'I'll be at the sheriff's office up in Saint

155

George in about three days. You fellows meet me there and we'll make out the papers for your claim on Hampton's bounty ... Unless you figure to stay down here and try for some wild horses. I'll have the papers signed and waiting, whenever you get up there.'

Reg looked pained. 'Marshal, I don't care if I never seen another wild horse as long as I live.'

Tetford's steady blue eyes showed a faint glint of amusement, but he did not pursue that topic. As he was arising he said, 'It'll take at least three days to get up there with the wagon. If I'm not there on time, lie around a little and wait.'

Lew nodded, put aside his tin plate and also arose. As they watched Marshal Tetford walk back over where the Seward sheriff was talking to a pair of his possemen, Reg said, 'I remember being wrong once before in my life. I was seven years old.'

Lew laughed. 'He's not a likeable man, for a fact, but he's sure good at his business ... Let's get our horses.'

It was still cool when they departed, their leave-taking hardly noticed by the busy possemen and the dispirited prisoners. They were a half-mile out when Tom twisted to glance back as he said, 'Hey; that sheriff won't have an accident with them Messicans will he?'

Lew and Reg exchanged a furtive glance. Reg said, 'Tom, was that the truth what you told us about your grandfather being shot by a firing

156

squad up at Mountain Meadows?'

Lee straightened forward. 'I'd have no reason to make up that story, Reg. He was shot up there and y'know, it was twenty years to the day from when he set up that massacre of all those emigrants ... Right down to the little kids.' Tom rode in silence for about a half-mile before speaking again. 'You know how many wives my grandpaw had? Twenty. One time he married three ladies in one day.'

What had begun as a ruse to divert the big Mormon from what the Seward sheriff might do to his Mexican prisoners, had now become more of a diversion for Lew and Reg. They rode along in the direction of the horse camp staring at Lee.

Finally, Reg said, 'How many kids did he have, Tom?'

Lee was uncertain. 'I think maybe about a hunnert ... I never knew him. He was killed long before even my maw grew up and got married.' Tom saw their expressions, and smiled. 'Can you imagine a man havin' twenty wives at one time?'

They couldn't, and although Reg eventually either forgot or lost interest in this affair, Lew never did, and many years after the last time he saw Tom Lee up in Saint George, Utah, wanting to test the veracity of the big Mormon, he researched John Doyle Lee. Tom had not only told the truth, but his grandfather had done much more than Tom had known about.